LOVE ME FOR WHO I AM

JUDY BARNES

ISBN
978-1-959365-00-6 (Paperback)
978-1-959365-01-3 (eBook)

TABLE OF CONTENTS

PREFACE

This book is totally fiction. None of the people are real. This manuscript came to my mind and I felt inspired to write it. Any names or places that sound familiar are all made up because of my interest in writing.

I haven't any basis for the content. Anything you read came from my brain and as much inspiration as came to me.

I am interested in people from all walks of life. I don't mean to judge anyone. I love everyone I have ever known. Please forgive me if I have stepped on anyone's toes. It was unintentional.

I have written other books. Hopefully, you have read them, especially my trilogy; Two Girls From Nazareth, Born to Be King of the World and His Unconditional Love.

I hope you will enjoy LOVE ME FOR WHO I AM. I've tried to look at the material from other points of view.

Judy Barnes

DEDICATION

This book is dedicated to the millions of wonderful people, no matter who you are or how you feel about those you think of as being different.

I have a philosophy that we are all different in a unique way. I don't believe that any one is normal. I believe that we are all normal in our own way. Please look on this book as your own kind of normal.

CHAPTER
ONE

"Tom, wake up!" Janet exclaimed loudly. "I think it is time to go to the hospital."

The father-to-be turned toward his hysterical wife. "Are you sure? This is not one of your false alarms."

"No, this is different. I've never had this sensation before. I'm having hard contractions about ten minutes apart"

Janet nudged her husband who was trying to go back to sleep. TOM, will you listen to me? This is the real thing."

"I will call the doctor. You get my suitcase from the closet."

"You get dressed. I'll put my bathrobe and slippers on."

"Janet, it's freezing out there. The roads are covered with snow," he said as he was looking out the window. "We both better get our heavy jackets and boots on. Get your purse, I'll take your suitcase."

"Here, let me help you down the stairs. I'll put your things in the car and start it. You stay by the door and I'll come and help you to the car."

"Tom, I haven't called the doctor yet."

"His number is right by the phone, isn't it?" Tom asked.

She waddled to the phone and picked up the receiver. Each number clicked as she dialed the doctor's answering service. "This is Janet Williams. I have gone into labor and we are leaving for the hospital."

"I will let Dr. Lewis know", was the response on the other end of the line.

* * * * *

Tom was heard to say, "Let me help you, Janet. We need to be on our way."

"I'm not an invalid, you know", Janet replied.

"I know, but it is slippery out here and I wouldn't want you to fall."

Janet said, "You are so thoughtful."

Tom put his right arm around her waist and held her hand tight as they walked carefully to the car.

She slipped into the front passenger seat.

Tom asked, "Are you ok?"

"I am snug as a bug in a rug", she answered. They both snickered.

Another contraction began as the car slowly backed out of the garage. Janet winced a bit. She didn't want to alarm her husband. She figured he was already nervous. She was!

The road was slippery, so they had to go a little slower than usual. Each time he tried to speed up a little, the car would slide one way or the other. It seemed like it was taking forever to reach their destination.

Finally, they could see the name of the hospital in bright red letters; RODCHESTER MEMORIAL HOSPITAL.

Janet relaxed a little. She hadn't realized the tense feeling in her hands and back.

* * * * *

Tom carefully pulled up to the Emergency Entrance. He couldn't believe how much it had snowed since they had gone to bed. He got out of the car and almost slipped in the fresh, white, wet snow.

He opened the door on the passenger side and helped his wife out of the car. An orderly was waiting with a wheel chair to take her to Admittance. Tom retrieved her items from the back seat.

He waited a few minutes to find out where Janet had been taken. Then he proceeded to find a parking spot.

Tom scurried back inside to the Admittance area.

Janet had just been wheeled to the first cubicle.

The woman behind the desk was all business. "Your name?"

"Janet Williams"

"Do you have your insurance card?" the lady asked.

Janet handed her the card.

"Is everything on the card correct?

"Yes, of course."

"What is your doctor's name?"

"Dr. Simon Lewis"

"Has he been called?" the receptionist asked.

"Yes, I called him before we left the house" Janet returned.

The lady picked up the phone and called for an orderly to take her up to Maternity. Then she put the wristband with all of the information on Janet's wrist.

By this time Tom was getting anxious. What was taking so long? What if she has the baby in the hallway? What if the doctor doesn't get here in time? What if there were complications?

Janet seemed very calm. She knew she was where she belonged. She was confident Dr. Lewis would be there in plenty of time.

The orderly arrived to transport the expectant mother to the fourth floor.

Janet felt like the contractions were becoming more frequent and harder.

She was wheeled into room 412. She really didn't care. All she wanted to do is lie down on a bed. She was tired of sitting in the wheelchair. The orderly helped her out of her jacket and onto the bed. She wished the doctor would hurry. She felt like she were going to panic, but she didn't want to in front of Tom. She needed to be calm in front of him. She knew that if she panicked, then he would start to panic too.

Just about that time, Dr. Lewis walked into the room. "Hi, Janet. I see you are being well taken care of. How are you Tom?"

"Nervous!" Tom exclaimed. "Do all new fathers feel this way, or am I reacting badly?"

"Tom, you are perfectly normal. Just try to relax."

The doctor examined the expectant mother. "Relax and try to get some rest. It will be a while before your son or daughter will make his or her entrance into this new world."

Janet had a frown on her face. "I'll be glad when this is over. I don't want to rest. I want this baby."

"Patience, my dear. Babies take their own time. We just have to relax. The father looks relaxed."

Janet glanced at Tom, who had leaned back in the chair, folded his arms and was snoozing."

"It must be nice. He's not the one having contractions seven minutes apart."

Dr. Lewis let out a quiet giggle and exited the room.

The mother said, quite loudly, "Tom, if you think you are going to sleep while I'm in agony, you're wrong. Wake up and keep me company."

"Mmmmm hmmm." He was out to the world.

Janet laid quietly fuming.

* * * * *

Dr. Lewis came in on the half hour. "There has been very little progress. You have a stubborn little one."

Next half hour about the same. Half hour number three she had dilated to five. Ten seemed a long way away.

The Doctor announced, "First babies quite often take their time. After all it's nice and warm in there."

* * * * *

Right at three o'clock on the button, Janet's water broke with a gush. She pushed the button for the nurse. About two minutes later the nurse arrived. Sure enough, Janet's water had erupted. It seemed like a tsunami to her. It was a gush, all at once.

"I can feel the baby coming" Janet remarked.

Dr. Lewis reminded her, "You have plenty of time. It may be another hour or two."

"Please, Dr. Lewis, will you check. I'm sure I can feel the head."

Dr. Lewis pushed the sheet back and gave a gasp, "You are right. I can see the baby's head. We don't have time to get you to the delivery room." He fumbled for his surgical mask and gloves. The baby was going to make its entrance NOW!

Tom felt as if he were going to faint. All of the color was gone from his face.

"Tom, you are going to have to help. Nurse, get him scrubbed and help him with a mask and gloves."

"Yes, Doctor. Come Mr. Williams, let's get started."

By the time Tom was in a gown, in gloves and with a surgical mask on, the baby was screaming.

"Tom, you have a fine baby boy. You can hold him as soon as the nurse has him cleaned up. Yes, a fine baby boy", Dr. Lewis said proudly.

"But I didn't do anything", Tom acknowledged.

"Nature took care of itself. Yes, a fine baby boy", the doctor reiterated.

The nervous father looked at his wife, "How are you."

Janet was smiling. "I'm just fine. We have such a handsome baby, I think we should name him Thomas Allen Williams, Jr. We can call him Tommy."

"He should always give you the credit for his upbringing. He will always have only the best in this life", Tom, Sr. relayed to his wife.

* * * * *

In a few minutes, Dr. Lewis came into the room. He was frowning. "I have some bad news to tell you."

Right away, Tom almost screamed, "Is the baby alright?"

"Yes, your son is fine. However I have some bad news." He looked disgruntled. "Janet, in the process of your baby's birth, there was a small tear in the uterus. We had to remove your uterus as soon as we were able to transport you to the operating room. I'm sorry, but you will not be able to have any more children."

Tom and Janet both felt remorse, but at least Tommy was healthy.

Tommy had the best care in the hospital.

* * * * *

Today was the day that he was taken to his new home. Tom had made sure he had the best money could buy. There was nothing too good for Tommy.

* * * * *

Tom and Janet owned a large dairy farm. It was a lot of work, but Tom had hired some men to help with the work of taking care of three hundred milk cows and half a dozen bulls. There were machines to put on the cows that milked them automatically. But there was a lot more to taking care of and seeing to it that the cows got milked. They have to be taken out to pasture every morning, the barn had to be cleaned out and fresh hay and other feed had to be put into the proper places so the cows could eat. And water needed to be filled into the water containers so the animals can maintain good hydration.

It takes many people to run a successful dairy farm.

Besides the numerous bovine, Janet had about a hundred free range chickens. The eggs were a profit for Janet. Now that Tommy had been born, she hired help to take care of the chickens, eggs, and chicks that came along. There is a lot more to taking care of chickens than just going out to pick up the eggs every day. They had to be fed, watered, and their living areas cleaned out every day. The help had to know how to get the chickens ready for market. With Tommy home, Mama doesn't have much time to take care of chickens, chicks, and eggs. One of the women, Connie, brought the eggs to Janet in a basket.

* * * * *

Tommy was a happy, healthy baby until he was about three months old.

One morning just before Mama was ready to get Tommy up for the day, she heard him coughing. His cough was getting worse by the minute. She picked him up and patted him on the back. He started crying and coughing, at the same time. Harder by the minute.

She tried to get in touch with Tom, but he was somewhere in the field tending to new born calves.

Finally, she called Tommy's Pediatrician, Doctor James, "Tommy is coughing and having a hard time breathing. I keep patting him on the back, but that doesn't seem to help. He just keeps coughing and crying."

She was starting to panic.

The receptionist on the other line of the phone responded, "Mrs. Williams, we can get Tommy in about 2:00 this afternoon. Will that be alright?"

Now Janet was really panicking, "No, you don't understand, I need to get him into see Dr. James NOW!

"I'm sorry, Mrs. Williams, we don't have any openings until 2:00."

"I can't wait until 2:00. He needs to see a doctor right away."

"Mrs. Williams, it won't do you any good to panic and get upset."

The receptionist could hear Tommy crying and coughing in the background. "I think you should take him to the hospital right away. It sounds like he might have Croup. There is no way we can get him into the office before this afternoon. Please take my advice and take him to the hospital right away!" the receptionist said sympathetically.

"Thank you, I will take him right away." Janet was beginning to calm down. That idea was making sense.

She called her helper. "Connie, I have to take Tommy to the hospital right now. Please send word to Mr. Williams, by one of the hired hands, to meet me there."

Connie smiled and went toward the barn so the message from Mrs. Williams could be relayed.

* * * * *

Janet changed Tommy's diaper and retrieved a bottle from the fridge. She bundled him up, grabbed the car keys and her purse and proceeded to the car. She was calm. She knew everything was going to be fine as soon as she could get Tommy to Emergency at the hospital.

* * * * *

Janet went down the snowy road to the hospital. The traffic was light. She drove as cautiously as she could. She saw emergency vehicles up ahead with their lights glaring in the sunlight.

She got as close as she could. A policewoman walked up to the car and motioned for Janet to roll down her window. "Ma'am, you can't get through here. There has been an accident up ahead. You must turn around and go down Fisher Road to Adams Avenue, then turn right and that will take you back to the Highway."

"Officer, I must get my son to the hospital. He is very sick."

"Ma'am, it will take you longer if you try to go this way. Please go back to Fisher Road and turn right on Adams Avenue, then turn right and it will take you back to the Highway. That will be the quickest way." She smiled a knowing smile.

Janet smiled back and thanked the police woman. She realized she was only doing her job. She turned around and went the way the officer suggested.

She followed the instructions and was at the hospital as quickly as possible. When she arrived, she saw an ambulance at the entrance. That was probably from the accident she had come upon.

Janet found a parking space and got the baby out of the car and walked carefully to the Emergency Entrance. The person from the ambulance was already inside.

Tommy wasn't crying, but he was still coughing. A man met them at the door and directed her to a waiting area. Janet sat with Tommy resting his head on her shoulder. His coughing slowed down but never completely stopped. She waited patiently. She could see they were busy.

About a half hour later Tom arrived. "Sorry I couldn't get here sooner. I came as soon as I got the message. What's going on?"

"Nothing really. We're still waiting to be seen."

"I didn't know he was sick. If I had known, I wouldn't have left the house", Tom said apologetically.

"I didn't know either until I heard him coughing about the time I was going to get him up. When he didn't stop coughing I decided to get him to the hospital as soon as I could. There was an accident on the Highway, so I had to detour. The traffic was not bad so I was able to get back on the Highway soon. I got here about the same time as the ambulance with the injured person from the wreck."

"I called the doctor's office first. They couldn't get Tommy in until this afternoon. The receptionist suggested I take Tommy to the hospital. I think that was a wise move", Janet explained.

Tom explained, "I just wish I could have gotten here sooner."

"That's not important. You're here now."

A call was heard from one of the cubicles, "Thomas Williams come to number 5."

Tom and Janet rushed Tommy to the appointed place.

"What is the problem," a nice lady asked with a smile.

"Tommy has been coughing ever since he woke up this morning."

"Did you call the Pediatrician?"

"Of course. They could not see him until this afternoon and I didn't think, we should wait. I wanted him seen as soon as possible," the mother said.

"We'll need to see his insurance card and have his doctor's name." The lady wrote all of the information in the typewriter and then put his identification wrist band on his arm. "Have a seat over there and someone will call for him when they are ready" The lady smiled as she pointed to the seating area.

In about ten minutes a man called out, "Thomas Williams?"

His parents stood and followed the man to a small room.

"Wait here, Doctor Andrews will be here shortly.

When the doctor came in, he used his stethoscope to listen to Tommy's chest and back. "There's a lot of congestion in his lungs. I'd like to keep him overnight. We'll put him on a respirator and give him some antibiotics.

We'll keep close watch over him to be sure it doesn't go into pneumonia. Someone will come and take him to a room upstairs."

"Doctor, I want to stay with him." Janet announced.

"We'll arrange for a cot to be brought in for you."

"Thank you. I don't feel good about leaving him."

* * * * *

The night was uneventful. Janet hated seeing him with all of the tubes and apparatus on him, but she knew it was for his own good. She was just thankful she was there and Tommy would realize that Mama was there. She wasn't able to hold him, but he was able to wrap his little hand around her finger. His coughing wasn't as bad. Hopefully he would be able to go home tomorrow. The nurse came in every half hour and checked his vitals.

About 9:00 in the morning, Dr. Andrews came in and announced that Tommy would be released. The baby had a cold, so he could go home along with ten days supply of anti-biotics and some vitamins.

Tom came to take them home at 10:15.

TWO

At six months, Tommy was beginning to sit up by himself. Mama would sit him on a blanket in the middle of the floor and he would hold himself up for a couple of minutes and then he would tip over. He would laugh and try to sit himself up.

Janet laid him down on his stomach with some of his toys in front of him. She turned her back, just for a moment, and when she looked again, he was sitting up. He reached for his favorite toy and looked up a Mama and laughed.

She couldn't wait to tell Daddy that Tommy sat up by himself.

When Tom came in that late afternoon, he didn't believe that Tommy had sat up by himself. He said, "I don't think he is supposed to sit up by himself at six months. Is he?"

"I think that is the normal time for him. Tom, he is so proud of himself. Every time he sits up, he laughs."

Sure enough, when Tommy sat up, he laughed. Mama and Daddy watched him. They couldn't help it, they laughed with him. The more they laughed, the more he laughed.

They thought he was an amazing baby.

* * * * *

On his first birthday, Tom and Janet invited all of their relatives they have, over. Mom made a beautiful cake and bought some ice cream. There were about 15 people in attendance. When the gifts had been opened and everyone was eating, Aunt Mary looked at Tommy and exclaimed, "Look at Tommy, he's standing."

Tommy got scared because of the excitement. He sat down and started crying.

Mama picked him up and patted him on the back. He calmed down and laid his head on his mother's shoulder. He was getting tired. It had been an exciting, long day. Janet sat in her favorite chair with Tommy on her lap. He was soon sleeping soundly.

The company started leaving, going to Janet to say goodbye so she would not have to get up. Everyone quietly retreated out the door with big smiles on their faces. Tommy was definitely the star attraction.

* * * * *

A couple of days after his birthday, he started walking. Now he could get into everything.

Mama had to think up ideas to keep him busy. She started going to the yard to pick up eggs. He thought that was lots of fun. He found that he could pick up the eggs and throw them. He laughed out loud when they would break.

Janet decided she had better look for a different game.

She decided to let him help her make cookies. He loved cookies. When you are making cookies, you don't let helpers near the flour. When she finished putting the dough together, there was flour all over the counter top and all over the floor.

Now what? Maybe he could help vacuum the floor. The only problem was that he couldn't move fast enough. It took too long to get the floor clean.

Next she took him out on the porch and swept the dirt and leaves off. He thought it was great fun to play with the leaves.

She was so so ready for naptime. Not just for Tommy, but also she needed to rest for a while. She didn't know that a one year old could have so much energy. She could hardly keep up with him.

THREE

Tommy had his third birthday. He was tall for his age and very happy. He got a lot of presents from family and friends. He received several large trucks. He received a dump truck, 2 semi-trucks, and a pick-up truck. They were nice but he didn't want to play with them. He lined them up on a shelf in his room. He also received many cars. All little boys like cars. He also lined them up on his shelf.

He took books and pretended to read them. That was what he enjoyed the most. The Adventures of Alice in Wonderland, Braer Bear, and others like that. Mama had read them to him many times. He almost could recite them word for word. He would look at the pictures and remember what Mama had read to him.

Daddy didn't understand why he was interested in books and not trucks and cars.

Mama was thrilled that he wanted to read. She would sit with him for hours reading to him and pointing to each word as she read. Tommy would get excited when she pointed to a word he recognized. He seemed awfully young, however, Mama knew he was learning to read.

When Mama was making cakes and cookies and brownies, Tommy wanted to be in the kitchen and help. He would help beat the desserts, following Mama's instructions. She was careful so he wouldn't get hurt. Quite often he made a mess, but Mama showed him how to clean up after himself. He learned how to put the batter in the cake pans, how to put the cookies on the baking pans. He loved helping Mama.

When Daddy came in from taking care of things on the farm, he was disturbed to find his son helping in the kitchen.

They had a discussion after Tommy went to bed.

Tom started, "I think I will take Tommy to work with me tomorrow. I want him to see what Real Men do during the day."

"But Tom, he is just a little boy. He likes helping Mama around the house. I don't think it is harming him to see the chores I do each day. But if you think he would enjoy seeing you at work, I think that would be great."

* * * * *

Work on a large milk farm starts really early.

Mama woke Tommy up about 4:30 a.m.

The boy started whining. "I don't want to get up. I'm still tired."

"Breakfast is ready. Daddy wants you to go with him this morning so you can learn what Daddy does all day." She started getting him dressed in blue jeans and a warm shirt. She put his sox and boots on him and led him to the kitchen.

"I don't want to help Daddy. I want to stay here with you", Tommy said in his whiniest voice.

"Be a good boy and go with Daddy today. Just think, you can see all of the cows getting milked and the big tank truck that comes and gets the milk to take to the milk plant to be made safe for big boys like you to drink. Then it is bottled and taken to grocery stores to get sold."

"Do I have to go?"

"It will make Daddy happy to have his big helper today." Mama had a big smile on her face to reassure her son that he was going to have a good time.

Daddy came into the kitchen. He had a big grin as he said, "There's my big boy. I'm so glad you are going with me today."

"Do I have to go?" Tommy said sounding as unhappy as he was able.

"We're going to have such a good time. You will be my big helper", Tom said trying to make it sound like such a great adventure.

"But Mama needs me here to help her", the boy stated.

"Did she tell you she needed you to stay with her?" Was the reply to the young boy.

"No, but I just know she does. She always tells me what a big help I am to her", the boy said.

Mama looked at Tommy and said, "Daddy would like you to see the kind of work he does. Just think, you can ride in his big truck."

He looked warily at his mother, "If you think it's ok."

"It will be lots of fun. You'll see." She smiled the biggest smile she was able.

The family ate their breakfast and Tom took his son by the hand and led him to the back door and put his heavy jacket on him. Tommy was still apprehensive. He didn't know how hard work could be fun. He had always been told that Daddy worked hard. He turned and waved to Mama as he went out the door.

The barn seemed a long way from the house. They went downstairs where the cows were. It didn't smell very good. Tommy pinched his nose.

"First, we have to give the cows some hay. He took a pitch fork and started giving each cow some of the hay from the bale that he took to each bovine. Tommy picked up some hay in his hands and took it to the next cow. Tom was pleased to see how his son was helping.

"What do you do next?" Tommy asked. He was getting bored distributing the hay.

"Next, we get some warm soapy water and wash the teats so we can attach the milking machines to each cow's udders. We have many people that help the cows get milked. I can see we need to move on to something else.

We'll leave the milking to our other men and women."

"Ladies help in milking the cows?" Tommy asked.

"Yes, Tommy, we have many ladies helping in different areas on the farm."

Next, Tom put Tommy in the truck and they rode out to where the feed gets distributed to the cows after they have been milked.

Tommy watched as some trucks let feed out of some trucks. He liked seeing the cows follow behind the trucks eating the feed.

"Why doesn't this truck let out feed for the cows to eat?"

"We have special trucks to feed the cows in the field," Daddy said.

Tom took the boy where some fences were being mended so the cows couldn't get out. Tommy thought that was good, but he was getting tired. He laid down on the truck seat and started to fall asleep. Tom figured it was time to take the boy back to the house. This was too much for one days outing.

Back at the house, Daddy carried the boy inside to the waiting arms of his mother.

She took him to his bed and laid him down for a good nap.

Tom was waiting for her return. "I think he is too young to realize the work that goes into running a dairy farm."

"I was sure of it. He's contented with the things he can do to help me."

"Maybe in another year or two", Tom said as he sulked out the door.

* * * * *

Tom came to the house all excited. He had had an idea.

"Tommy, let's get your trucks and cars and play with them".

"No, Daddy, I want to help Mama make biscuits. She told me she would let me help."

Daddy sulked and went into the living room to read the newspaper.

Mama said, "Wouldn't you like to play with Daddy? He would love to play with you."

"I want to help you. Can I stay with you and help you make supper?"

Exasperated, Mama breathed a big sigh and continued making the biscuits for supper.

After supper, Tom and Janet sat at the table while Tommy colored some pages in his color book. "Janet, I don't know what to do. I want Tommy to spend some time with me so he can learn what a man does."

"I know, Tom, but he is just a little boy. He doesn't know what he wants to do. Helping me around the house and coloring in his books is mostly what he wants to do right now. Maybe when he is in school and plays with children his own age, he will discover new avenues to travel on."

Tom smiled at the analogy and just shook his head. "I wonder if he would like me to read him his bedtime story. I'll look through his books and see if there is one he hasn't heard a dozen times."

Janet responded, "It's worth a try."

* * * * *

Tom went to his son's bedroom and looked through his library of children's books. He pretty much knew the ones Janet had read to him. He said to himself, "I've never heard him mention Carz. I'll start with that one." He took it off the shelf and put it beside his bed.

"Tommy, Daddy is going to read to you at bedtime tonight", Mama said with enthusiasm.

"Okay", the boy said as he rubbed his eyes.

Tom picked up his son and took him upstairs to his bedroom. He helped the boy take off his daytime clothes and helped him on with his pajamas. Then he proceeded to take the book he had selected for his bedtime story.

Tommy snuggled in his blankets and awaited the story.

Daddy smiled at his son as he sat on the edge of the bed with the book securely in his hands. He turned the book so Tommy could see the front of the book.

"That's not the book I wanted you to read to me", Tommy whined.

"Look, Son, it's the one about Carz", Daddy tried to sympathize.

"But, I want the one about the Bear and Eeyore. I like the Honey Jar. I don't want to hear the one about Carz." He turned over and covered his head and pretended to go to sleep.

Daddy was frustrated. Why was he not able to satisfy a little four year old boy?

Tom walked to the door and turned out the light. He left the door part way open.

He walked down stairs to the living room where Janet was watching television.

"I don't know what to do. Anything I want to do with Tommy always ends in disaster. He doesn't want to do anything I want to do. Doesn't he realize he is a boy? Why does he want to cook and clean house? Why isn't he interested in boy things, like trucks, cars, airplanes, farming?"

"Honey, sit down beside me. Maybe I can explain a few things. He has always been around me. He sees the things I do every day. He wants to help me. Most of the greatest chefs are men. Be happy that he wants to keep things clean and tidy. Most boys his age can't even pick up after themselves."

"Tom, you are always too busy with the farm to pay attention to our boy. Yes, you took him out with you one day. There really wasn't anything for him to do except follow you around. That must be awfully boring for a four year old who doesn't understand how important your job is."

Tom just stared into space, trying to absorb what Janet was saying; trying to make sense of the whole conversation.

"I'm sure you are right. When he is eight we can sign him up for soft ball, football and basketball. Maybe some of his friends will be in sports and can interest him in them." Tom was daydreaming about the day when his son would be in the Olympics, or on a Major League Team. Yes his son would be one of the 'Greats'. Until that time he would try to interest him in sports young boys could participate in.

* * * * *

He decided to take a little time off and go into town. The sporting goods store was his destination. He bought a bat and softball. And a little bigger ball to practice catch with.

When he got home, Tommy was naturally going around the living room trying to dust everything he could reach.

"Tommy, would you like to go outside and play catch with Daddy?" Tom asked with great enthusiasm.

"No, Daddy. I want to finish dusting", Tommy remarked and smiled.

"But Tommy, I thought it would be fun if we could play catch together."

"I have to dust the rest of the furniture. I don't know how to play catch."

"That's a fun game that boys can play with their fathers. I went to the store and bought a new bat and softball and a ball that would be easy to learn to catch", Tom remarked, trying to entice the boy into learning to play with his Dad.

"How about if I help you dust and then we can play catch outside until supper time?" Tom suggested.

"Is Mama fixing supper? Maybe she would need my help" Tommy thought out loud.

Tom thought, 'That was a stupid idea.'

"How about after supper?" was the question. "I would really like to play catch with you."

Mama, hearing the conversation said, "That sounds like a great idea."

"Okay," Tommy said reluctantly.

* * * * *

When supper was finished, Tom took his son by the hand and led him to the back yard.

He instructed the boy to hold his hands in front of him to try to catch the ball. He did as he was told, however, the ball hit Tommy in the leg. He let out a yell. "That hurt, Daddy. I want to go in the house."

Tom remarked, "Let's play a little longer. I think you'll get the hang of it."

I don't like this game. My leg hurts. I think we have played this game long enough."

Tom walked with his arm around Tommy's shoulder into the house. When in the house, the boy ran to the living room and started watching the World News.

Tom said to Janet, "I don't know what to do. He doesn't want to do anything with me."

"Why don't you ask him what he would like to do with you?" was Janet's idea.

Tom responded with, "I'll try anything."

Janet smiled.

* * * * *

Tommy awoke all excited for the new day. He called out to Mama, "Can I take a bath before breakfast?"

Janet was inquisitive, "Of course. Why can't you wait until after breakfast?"

"I feel like doing something different."

"Okay", Janet said as she raised one eyebrow."

She led the boy into the bathroom and turned the water on. Then she went into Tommy's bedroom looking for clothes for him. When she returned to the bathroom, Tommy was undressed and ready to climb into the tub. The water was a little bit too warm, so she turned the hot water off and only had the cold water on until the water was the right temperature.

Tommy climbed into the tub and smiled at Mama. "The water is just right."

"Let me know when you are ready to get out. I will come and dry you off with one of our big fluffy towels." She knew how much he liked the fluffy towels. They felt so good on his tender skin.

Tom had already gone to the barn to take care of the early chores. He told Janet that he would be back as soon as he was able.

It wasn't too long before Tommy was clean, dressed and rushing down stairs just ahead of Mama.

"I'm getting to be a big boy now. I can do things my way."

Mama asked, "What do you mean?"

"I can take my own bath and dress myself. Well, most of the time. You can help me with the things I have trouble with."

"I can tell you what I want for breakfast."

"That's true", Mama grinned at Tommy's new found decisions he had acquired.

"What would you like for breakfast?"

"Hmm, I think I would like two pieces of toast, and a big bowl of cereal", was his answer.

"I think you should decide between two pieces of toast and cereal", was the logical answer any mother would make.

"No, I would like two pieces of toast and a big bowl of cereal."

"Think about it for a minute. Two pieces of toast is good for a big boy like you. Or a bowl of cereal. Both would be too much and you would probably get a tummy ache."

"But Mama, I am a growing boy and I want a big breakfast so I can grow up to be as big as Daddy."

Janet thought she had come up with an appropriate solution. She went to the cupboard and took out two pieces of bread and put them into the toaster. Then she proceeded to the cupboard and retrieved a small bowl and then got out the box of cereal. She put the bowl and a spoon on the table and got the milk out of the refrigerator. She looked a little dubious. Toast and cereal?

The toaster popped up. She placed the toast on a small plate and proceeded to put butter on them.

Tommy exclaimed, "I want to do it myself."

"Okay, but I want to watch you so you don't get too much butter on the toast."

"I can do it."

Janet watched Tommy carefully. He did it by himself. He devoured the toast and proceeded to the task of putting the cereal and milk in the bowl. Mama sat down on a chair across from her son.

He put too much cereal in the bowl, but hurriedly picked up the extras and placed them back into the bowl.

"The milk is too heavy. Can you help me?"

Janet came around to his side of the table. She carefully lifted the container and Tommy put his hands on it too. Then she carefully poured a small amount of milk on the cereal.

"Thank you, Mama. It was too heavy."

"I know it was. I'm glad I was here to help you."

"I'm getting to be a big boy", Tommy said.

"Yes, you are. I'm so proud of you", was the reply. She was thinking, he's growing up too fast.

* * * * *

Tom came home about lunchtime. He immediately looked for Tommy. Of course, he was in the kitchen with Mama.

"Tommy, how would you like to spend the afternoon with Daddy?"

"I don't know. What are we going to do? I don't want to go to the barn", the boy said.

"Well, what would you like to do?" Dad asked.

"We could go out and hunt for eggs", Tommy suggested.

"Let's think of something fun. Would you like to go to a toy store and go shopping?" was another idea of Daddy's.

"That doesn't sound like fun. That's too much walking", Tommy remarked.

"How about going to the ice cream shop and getting a sundae or cone with lots of ice cream and sprinkles?" Daddy smiled.

"No, I don't want to go anywhere. I want to stay home." Tommy retaliated.

Tom was getting frustrated. "I wish we could do something together."

Tommy lit up, "Let's make a cake or cookies. Mama has been letting me help her. I like to make balls in my hands and put them on the pans. Mama won't let me put the pans in the oven. She's afraid I will get burned."

Dad returned with, "I don't know how to make cookies."

"That's ok, Mama can make the mix and you and I can make the balls and put them on the pans. Maybe Mama will let you put the pan in the oven."

Dad and Mama snickered.

"Mama, do you want to help Tommy and me make cookies?" Daddy asked.

"I don't know. I was planning on going to the grocery store and pick up a few things", Mama replied.

Tommy squealed with excitement, "Can Daddy and I go with you? I love to go shopping with you."

Tom looked disappointed. He wanted so much to spend time with his son alone.

Mama said, "Not this time. Today you should spend time with Daddy."

* * * * *

Janet fixed lunch and the family sat and ate sandwiches and potato chips, with cookies made yesterday for a treat.

When the kitchen was cleaned up, Mama put on her coat and was off to the market leaving Tom and Tommy to decide what kind of fun they could have.

About an hour later, she returned to find her men sleeping on the couch with the television blaring.

So much for an afternoon of fun. Janet turned the television down and retreated to the kitchen to put the groceries away.

CHAPTER
FOUR

Tommy turned five. Another birthday party. Grandpa and grandma, aunts and uncles, and lots of cousins were invited.

Tommy couldn't believe it. More cars and trucks, and baseball and mitt, and basketball along with a hoop that Daddy and Mama purchased.

Tommy thanked everyone for his gifts and went to his room. He looked out the window and watched his uncles and cousins playing with their items they brought from home. Daddy was putting the basketball hoop on the peak of the garage.

'Why can't I do the things I want to do on my birthday?'

* * * * *

Janet called everyone in for ice cream and cake. She even made chocolate milk shakes for everyone.

She called Tommy to come down.

"I don't want to", Tommy said.

"But it's your birthday. We would all like to have ice cream and cake with you", Mama said.

"I don't want any ice cream and cake. I want to stay in my room."

Aunt Mary commented, "What is wrong with that boy. Most boys can't wait for ice cream and cake on their birthday. You should make him come down."

"I don't know what is wrong with him. He just seems to want to do his own thing." Janet confessed.

"But he doesn't even play with his cousins. That's not natural." Uncle Pete remarked.

"I'm worried about him. He doesn't even enjoy being with his father." Janet stated.

"If he were my kid, I'd make him get into some kind of sports. He's going to be starting Kindergarten pretty soon, why not see if you can get him on a t-ball team. That way he would learn sportsmanship and what it means to be on a team where he would have to play with boys." Uncle Pete stood back and grinned. He surely knew how to raise a boy. He had five. He was one proud father.

Tom stroked his chin thoughtfully. That sounded like a great idea. He would look into that tomorrow.

The birthday party seemed to be a bust. Everyone went home early. The cousins were not happy because it was Tommy's birthday and he wouldn't even play with them.

Janet made Tommy come down and thank everyone for his gifts. He didn't even know or care who gave him what.

He thanked everyone half-heartedly. Everyone knew Janet had made him come down. When everyone was gone, he retreated back to his room, to look out the window and sulk. This was the worse birthday anybody could ever have.

* * * * *

After a good nights sleep, everyone was back to the old routines.

Tommy was helping Mama fix breakfast. Today was cereal day. That was easy. Bowls, knives and spoons were neatly arranged by Tommy. Mama set out juice glasses for the beverage. Mama put bread into the two-slotted toaster. Two minutes later, 2 scrumptious pieces appeared.

"Mama, can I just have toast and jelly for my breakfast?"

The reply was, "Wouldn't you like a nice bowl of cereal".

"No, I just want toast and jelly." Tommy grinned.

"Okay, then. Toast and jelly. Would you like orange juice too?"

"No, Mama, just toast and jelly."

"Are you sure that will be enough?" Mama asked.

"Yup, I'm not very hungry."

Tommy and Mama got the kitchen cleaned up and went outside to gather eggs.

"I like working with you. I want to work with you forever," The boy related.

"Someday when you are big, you will have to get a job, earn money and get an apartment of your own. Then when the right girl comes along, you will want to get married and have children."

"Girls are yucky. I don't like girls."

"You will like girls someday. You will think they are beautiful."

"Like you, Mama? I think you are beautiful."

Janet blushed, "You will see a girl and think she is the most beautiful girl you have ever seen."

"No girl will ever be as beautiful as you are. Can I marry you?"

"Sorry Bub, I'm already taken. Daddy and I are married."

"Why didn't you wait until I was big?"

"Your Daddy and I were married before you were born."

"That doesn't make sense. How could you be married before I was born?"

Janet was perplexed. How far should she go?

"You're supposed to get married and then have children."

Tommy was confused, but didn't ask any more questions.

* * * * *

Tom came home early. "I signed you up to be on a t-ball team."

"What is a t-ball team?"

Tom explained, "A group of boys get together and become a team. Then they practice hitting a ball off of a short pole. Then the boy who hit the ball runs to first base."

Being confused seemed to become natural for Tommy. "What is a base? Do you pick the base up?"

"There is a t-ball game tomorrow. We will go and watch."

"Okay", was the response.

* * * * *

Dad came in about 4:30. "Come son we need to leave. The t-ball game starts at 5:00."

"But we haven't had supper yet."

"That's okay, we can eat when we get home," Daddy replied.

Tom took Tommy's hand and led him to the car.

"How far is it, Daddy?"

"Not far."

Both were quiet until they reached their destination.

"There are a lot of kids. What if they don't like me?" Tommy asked.

"I'm scared."

"There's nothing to be scared about. They are all little boys about your age."

"I'm not sure about this," Tommy related.

"Just give it a try, please."

"Okay, but if I don't like it, I want to go home."

"Deal," Daddy said enthusiastically.

The two of them sat on the benches and watched the little boys hit the ball on a pole and run fast to first base. The ball was thrown by the pitcher to the base, but overthrew it.

"See Son, you can have a good time even if you don't hit the ball every time", Daddy said, trying to make Tommy see what fun the boys were having. "Wouldn't it be great to be out there with kids your own age, having fun?"

"I don't think so. I think I should stay home with Mama."

"Tommy, I would like you to pick a sport where you could meet other boys and have fun. Mama and I would come to all of your games to cheer you on. Wouldn't that be fun?"

"Are you sure Mama would come and watch me? Do you think she would like to see me hit the ball and run?'

"I think she would love to watch you."

Daddy was starting to get excited. Hopefully we've found something Tommy can do, to get him out of the house and playing with other children. He couldn't wait to get home to tell Janet.

"First, we will have to sign you up and get some equipment."

Tom found the man in charge so he could sign Tommy up to play t-ball. What an accomplishment. He was proud as a peacock.

He found Bill Adams and took Tommy with him. However, Bill was talking to someone else. He would have to wait a couple of minutes.

Finally, he could introduce himself and Tommy. "Hi Mr. Adams, I'm Tom Williams and this is my son Tommy. We would like to sign Tommy up for t-ball."

"I'm sorry, we don't need another player right now. However, we could use a water boy. Do you think he might be interested?"

Tom looked at his boy and could see the disappointment on his face.

"What do you think, Tommy? Would you like to be a water boy?"

"What does a water boy do?" Tommy asked as he looked at Mr. Adams.

"Well, it is an important job. You would have to make sure the boys had water to drink when they were done running around the bases. Do you think you could handle that?" Bill grinned as he spoke. "You would have to have a uniform like the rest of the boys."

Tommy's eyes lit up, "I think I could do that."

"Good, we'll see you tomorrow at 4:45 sharp so we can get a uniform on you and I can give you important instructions." Again Mr. Adams smiled. Tommy liked him.

Tommy was starting to feel important. He had a very important job.

Not a word was spoken all the way home. He was busy thinking about his new position on the t-ball team. He couldn't wait to tell Mama.

As soon as the car came to a stop in front of the garage, Tommy got out as quickly as he could, and ran to the house to find Mama.

As usual, she was in the kitchen getting supper on the table for her hungry men.

Tommy was so excited, his words seemed to come out jumbled.

"Slow down. Talk slowly so I can understand you."

"I got an important job with the team. I even get a uniform."

"What important job did you get?" Mama asked.

"I am the water boy. Isn't that great?"

Mama looked disappointed. Daddy noticed and shushed her right away.

"It's my job to see that the boys that are running around the bases have water, so they don't get too thirsty. I am very important."

Mama's attitude changed, "I think that is wonderful. You are very important. If you weren't there to give the boys water, they could get very sick."

"Will you come and watch me? I would really like it if you was there"

"Of course, I wouldn't miss it."

* * * * *

Tommy was water boy until he was too old to be on the team. He enjoyed it and thought the team couldn't get along without him.

He tried out for the baseball team when he was eight years old, but he hadn't had any practice in batting, hitting, running, and sliding into home. He decided he didn't want to play baseball.

Daddy took him aside and asked, "Do you know a game you would like to play? How about basketball or football? Those are fun games to play."

"I really am not interested in playing those games."

Back to the drawing board.

* * * * *

When he was 14 he needed more to do. He was too young to get a job, but he wanted to earn some money.

He was doing excellent in school. In fact, he was doing so good the principal asked if he would be interested in tutoring some students who are having trouble understanding English, Math, History or other classes.

"Yes, I could do that."

"Good, I will set up a schedule for you and a student will contact you to make arrangements for you to help him or her."

"Okay, I am looking forward to it."

He had always excelled in school. Now he was in the ninth grade and he felt confident that he could tutor other students.

About a week later a girl named Sharon Cooper set up an appointment with Tommy to help her with math. His dad took him to her house and picked him up when he was done.

Sharon really liked him and started talking about going out. "Do you think, maybe, we could go out to a movie or go for a soda sometime?"

"I'll have to ask my dad. I can't drive yet."

Sharon responded, "That would be fine. I don't care if your dad took us and picked us up."

"Okay, I'll ask him tonight and I'll let you know tomorrow when I come over for math."

Tom picked him up at the appointed time.

"Dad, do you think Sharon and I could go to the drug store for a soda sometime?"

"Do you like her?" was Dad's reply.

"Of course. I wouldn't be helping her with math if I didn't like her. She needs a lot of help and I can do it."

"Yes, but do you like her for more than just a student?"

"I don't know what you mean. She is just a student and a friend," Tommy returned.

"You don't feel anything romantical about her?" Dad quizzed.

"What do you mean?"

"Never mind."

Tom spoke to Janet privately. "Tommy wants to take a girl out for a soda sometime. I told him I would take them.

"That's wonderful. He's becoming interested in girls finally." Mom said.

"I'm not too sure. He didn't sound like he wanted to see her other than one time. I think it was her idea. He seems to be just interested in helping her with her math."

"We'll have to wait and see what happens." Tom explained.

FIVE

Tommy turned sixteen. There was a big celebration when he met that milestone. His grandparents, aunts and uncles and cousins were all there.

He greeted each person cordially and retreated to the porch to sit and watch the others have a good time.

His cousin Mickey approached him, "Tommy, come and play tag football with us. We could use another player."

"Thank you, but I think I will sit here and watch. I'm not really into sports."

"Please, we would love to have you join us."

"Maybe later." Was the only answer that would make Mickey leave him alone.

Uncle Pete came and sat beside Tommy. "Those kids seem to be having a good time. Wouldn't you like to be out there?"

"No, I can see all I want to from here. I'm glad they are having such a good time."

Uncle Pete continued, "Tell me a little about yourself. How is school?"

"Fine."

"I hear you have been tutoring for the past few years. That's terrific."

"Yeah, it keeps me busy."

"Are you in any sports at school?"

"No".

"Don't you like sports?"

"I've been thinking about trying out for the swim team."

"Swim team? Wouldn't you rather do something a little more rough? You know, like football or Soccer?"

"No."

Uncle Pete was getting nowhere with this conversation.

Aunt Harriet came and sat next to Tommy. "Do you have a girlfriend?"

"No."

"Isn't there any girls you are interested in?"

"No."

"How about male friends? You will be driving soon. Is there any place special you would like to go with your friends?"

"No."

So much for Aunt Harriet trying to strike up a conversation.

Tommy got up and went into the house. All of the women were in the kitchen, so he decided to watch television. There wasn't anything worth watching, so he went to his room.

He could hear the women talking, "What is wrong with Tommy. It's his birthday. You'd think he would want to hang around all of his cousins. He has gone to his room."

"I know," answered Janet. "He has always been somewhat of a loner. He doesn't have any friends, male or female. He says he just wants to be left alone and do his own thing."

"What is his own thing? Do you think he will look for a job? He has to do something other than stay in his room."

Janet sighed. "We don't know what to do for him. Any suggestions we make, he doesn't like."

Harriet started again, "Why doesn't he hang around any boys and especially girls. He's at that age, you know."

"He still is doing his tutoring. He seems to like that. He tutors both girls and boys. Anyone who needs his help."

"But he doesn't have a social life", Aunt Betty said.

"I know, but you can't push anyone to socialize."

Betty continued, "Has he been on any dates?"

"He took one of his students to the Malt Shop when he was in the ninth grade. Tom and Tommy picked her up and transported them to the Malt Shop. That was the only one."

"Doesn't he like girls?" Mary asked from out of nowhere.

"I guess he does. He's busy so much. I doubt he has anytime for girls or dating. Maybe he should stop and smell the roses."

Tommy quietly closed his bedroom door. He had heard enough.

* * * * *

After everything had been cleaned up, Tommy came down stairs and announced, "Mom and Dad I would like to be called TJ. Tommy sounds so juvenile."

"That's fine with me", Tom said.

"I understand completely," Janet agreed.

* * * * *

TJ started the eleventh grade. Everything seemed to be going well.

One night he confronted his parents when they were both in the living room watching the Olympics. "Mom, Dad, I think I would like to join the High School Swim Team."

Startled, both parents looked at each other. Dad started, "What brought that decision up?"

"You have always wanted me to be in sports. That is the only one I am truly interested in."

"I know," Tom continued, "But why swimming? I was hoping football, baseball, or basketball, even soccer."

"Swimming is the one sport I like. It's very versatile. There's several types of swimming. Then there's diving. There are a lot of meets, and maybe the Olympics." TJ grinned.

Tom looked perplexed. "Are you sure this is what you want?"

"I think that is something I would really excel at. I love to swim and if I could find a really good coach, who knows how far I could go."

Tom asked, "Is there a coach at school?"

"Yes," TJ answered. "But, if I am going to make a career out of this, I will have to have a professional coach. It could be pricy."

"Have you looked into getting a job? Not just as a tutor." His father ventured.

"Not seriously. I was waiting to get your opinion."

"Next year you will have to look into colleges that offer swimming as a career." Tom was getting very serious.

"Believe it or not," TJ started, "I have already looked into a few good colleges that offer swimming as a sport. Of course, I would also have to take some academic courses also. I don't think I would have any trouble getting into any college. My grades have been exemplary."

"I have also looked into grants to help with the cost. I really am serious about seeking a future in swimming. I understand that may not be the route you would have me go, but this is what I want. Please let me take my own route."

"Some colleges even give scholarships. I have even been approached by a couple of promising colleges." TJ explained.

"Why haven't you told us about this before?" His father asked.

"Well, I wanted to get a few thoughts together before I presented this idea to you," was TJ's reply.

"To be recruited for a men's college swimming team, high school student-athletes will need to put the same focus into their recruiting process as they do in improving their event times. Competing for a roster spot on a college team is daunting enough, and the competition for scholarships raises a lot of questions for the student-athletes and their families. In addition to maintaining good academic standing, student-athletes need to dedicate a lot of time and effort to both improving their swimming skills and proactively managing their own recruiting process."

"I can see you have been doing your homework," Dad said. "Why did it take so long for you to come to us?'"

"I didn't want to put the cart before the horse. I felt it would be better if I could present the whole program to you, so that you could see the progress I have been making." TJ admitted. "I still have a lot to do before I can be put on a list of coaches looking for examples as we find a college swimming program that is a great fit. We candidates have to look at all of the colleges we are interested in. Do I look for one close to home? Or do I look into an Ivy League College that might get me to my goal quicker. There are a lot of variables to consider."

Dad admitted, "I really didn't believe you were serious about taking swimming as a college program. I really admire you for all of the hard work you have done in getting this far. We will do all we can to help you in this endeavor. Let us know if there is anything at all we can do to help."

"Thank you, I think I have it all under control at this point. I appreciate the interest you are taking in my project. It means a lot to me." TJ smiled.

"I spoke to Coach Thompson the end of last year's school year and explained how I would like to get on the swim team this year. He watched me practice a few times. He gave me a few tips to help me improve my technique. I have followed all of his instructions. I can see improvement in myself. He has made sure I got on the team this year. If I keep improving, he said he would talk to some Coaches he knows and see if I can be advanced to the top team in High School and then recommend me to a few college coaches he knows. What a great opportunity that would be!"

"I am so proud of you for taking the initiative to check on the swimming team on your own. Most boys would have spoken to their parents first and then talked to Coach Thompson."

Janet stated, "We are both proud of you. You have always had excellent grades, even while tutoring other students."

"I won't be able to tutor anymore. I will have to spend every spare moment at school swimming. Coach Thompson said I won't have time for anything else. I am planning on going from my last class to the Gym to swim until about 10:00 p.m. Then I will come home and eat some supper if you will save some for me." TJ sneaked a grin at his mother.

"Of course I will. I will even sit with you while you eat." Mom said.

"Thank you Mom and Dad. You are the best parents in the world."

Janet blushed.

————

I received my information about Swimming Teams from the internet.

NCSA

Next College Student Athlete

Men's College Swimming Recruiting

Your Guide to Men's Swimming Recruiting

Men's swimming scholarships

# CHAPTER
SIX

Surprisingly, the swim team in TJ's high school was very large. He expected maybe five or six. Actually, there were twenty. That made it difficult to find a time to practice. It seemed the pool was always full with others waiting their turn.

TJ decided to go an hour before school started. Pretty much the same problem. Other students had the same idea. However, not quite as bad. He was able to eat his breakfast on the run. Part of his regimen was to run in order to keep strengthening his legs. He was able to eat, run, swim, shower, dress and get to his first class on time. He was becoming the athlete his father had always wanted him to be.

Janet was getting worried. Was he getting enough sleep? Was he eating enough? Was he able to keep up with all of his academics? She hardly ever got to see him, except at 10:00 at night when he came home for supper. She thought he was starting to look haggard.

"TJ, are you alright? You're burning the candle at both ends."

He replied, "I'm fine. Everything is fine. Please don't worry. I know I have to keep up this pace in order to reach my goal for this year."

"Okay, but are you going to have enough credits to graduate? When you are swimming day and night, when do you find time to study?"

"I have a 4.0 in all of my classes." TJ finished his meal, kissed his mother on the cheek and ran upstairs, changed into his pajamas and climbed into bed.

'Oh, for a good night's sleep. No more of the same dream.'

* * * * *

TJ was up at five, dressed and ran downstairs to grab his egg sandwich and swim bag and ran out the door. He got to the Gym door with time to spare, so he ran around the indoor track twice and then on to the pool.

There was only one person in the pool. Jackie was a good friend. He wouldn't mind if TJ swam next to him. Most of the guys treated TJ like he had some communicable disease. He couldn't figure out why.

When the guys talked about their girlfriends, he felt weird. He didn't have a girlfriend. He didn't have time. Jackie was his only friend. They ran together and swam together. Neither felt they had time for dating. Maybe someday.

* * * * *

Thanksgiving was coming fast. However, TJ and Jackie didn't change their routines at all. Running and swimming. That was their lives.

They were best friends. Where one was, you knew where the other one was. However, they both were living with their parents.

TJ asked, "Do you think it would be alright if I invite Jackie over for Thanksgiving Dinner?"

"Don't you think Jackie's parents would like him to be home for a big occasion like Thanksgiving Dinner? I wouldn't want you to go to someone else's home for Thanksgiving Dinner." Janet acknowledged.

"Okay, but it is going to be boring with our relatives here. There's nothing for me to do."

Janet answered, "With that many people here, I'm sure there will be plenty to do."

"Boring", TJ reiterated.

Dad asked, "TJ, would you like to help me set up tables? We're going to eat outside under that big Walnut tree."

"Sure, I wish I could go to the Gym and swim. This is going to be a long, long day." TJ meant every word. "I hate get togethers. Everyone has to be nice to each other. What a bunch of phonies."

Try to be cordial, TJ. You haven't seen your Grandma, Grandpa, Aunts, Uncles, or cousins in a long time. I'm sure they are anxious to hear about your swimming adventures. How you are going to a college that has a strong team," Tom said as he and TJ were putting the white tablecloths on each table.

"How many people are you expecting?"

Tom returned, "Probably around fifty. Your cousin Greg got married a couple of months ago. I'm sure they will be here."

As they were talking, the first of the guests arrived.

TJ continued the conversation, "Why would anyone want to get married that young? I want to wait until I am at least 25."

"That is the first time I have heard you speak of marriage," Tom said.

Uncle Pete and Aunt Mary walked up to greet the two who were setting up the tables.

"Hello, Tom. I see you and Tommy are doing a splendid job," Aunt Mary remarked.

Uncle Pete said, "You have really grown since the last time we saw you."

"Yes," Tom announced, "Our boy wants to be called TJ now. He feels he is too old to be called Tommy."

"Well, Tommy, Have you picked out a College yet?

"I've been considering Yale or maybe Princeton. They are both so chic." TJ turned and went into the house.

"Really, Tom, haven't you taught your boy any manners?" Mary asked.

About that time Grandma and Grandpa showed up in their new Lincoln.

They got out of their new car and walked up to the small group that was starting to form.

"Wasn't that Tommy we saw walking toward the house?" Grandpa asked. "I'm looking forward to playing touch football this afternoon."

"He wants to be called TJ. He's not really interested in touch football," Tom pointed out.

"I guess that's only right. He isn't a boy anymore," Grandma said as she got a faraway look on her face, as if remembering when he was just a little tot.

Soon, others arrived. Lots of cars and lots of people. All of the women congregated in the kitchen, while all of the men gathered on the porch to reminisce about past years. The cousins stood by the barn and tried to think of something fun to do.

TJ sat on the couch in the living room and watched absolutely nothing on television, wishing he was at the Gym swimming alongside Jackie. Then he heard the women cackling in the kitchen. "Is Tommy, sorry, TJ going to go to college next year?" Aunt Anita asked.

"Yes, he is in the process of picking one out now." Janet relayed.

"Is he going out for a sport? With his height, he would be good in either football or basketball, although he would have to put on a few pounds" Aunt Anita suggested.

"Actually, he is working on a scholarship right now. He wants to go out for swimming. He's been hoping to be recruited in one of the big colleges. He's even thinking of trying out for the Olympics. We are very proud of him."

Silence filled the kitchen. Not a sound was heard. Then Aunt Ellen said, "You're kidding, right? None of our boys even thought of going out for Swimming. Maybe you should have him checked out by a Psychologist. He must not be thinking straight."

"That's enough, Ellen. There is nothing wrong with becoming an Athletic Swimmer. He is being sought after by several Ivy League Schools. We're just waiting to see which one will be the right one."

* * * * *

TJ heard more than he wanted to. He went to his room, laid on his bed looking up at the ceiling. 'Is there something wrong with me? Why do people think there is something wrong with wanting to swim and look at it as an academic tragedy? I LIKE TO SWIM. I'll just stay in my room until everyone leaves.'

It wasn't long until he was asleep.

When he awoke, all he could think of was, "Oh no, not that dream again.'

'What does it mean.' He was still contemplating it's meaning, when he heard his mother call, "TJ, come and eat."

"I'm going to stay here. I'm not hungry."

"Please, Honey, Everyone is waiting for you."

Silence

Then father said, "TJ, Please come to dinner."

Silence

TJ could hear talking in the dining room, but he remained in his own compound. He didn't want to see anyone, talk to anyone, listen to anyone. He just wanted to be alone.

* * * * *

It was getting dark. He could smell popcorn popping. He knew everyone was watching home movies and having a good time. He didn't want any part of it.

It really did smell good. He missed not spending time with the family, but he didn't feel comfortable around any of them.

Something was definitely wrong.

* * * * *

TJ was still laying on his bed looking upward. He really couldn't be looking at anything. By now, his room was totally dark.

Then there was a soft knock on the door. "TJ, are you awake?"

"Yes, Mom."

"Can I come in?"

"Of course, Mom."

"Everyone is ready to leave and Dad and I thought it would be nice if you would come down and say 'Good-bye' to everyone."

"I really don't feel like seeing or talking to anyone."

"Do it for us. Just to be polite."

TJ placed his legs over the side of the bed and sat there for a couple of minutes. Then he raised himself into a standing position and walked toward the door.

"I'm only doing this for you and Dad. I would rather lay up here on my bed and forget the day."

"It's not that easy."

"I'm sorry, but we did the best we could to teach you manners and to be polite." Janet was standing with her arms folded, waiting for her son.

TJ quietly followed his mother down stairs. He was looking into the faces of about 47 blank faces. He did not like this one bit. He stood at the bottom of the stairs. Oddly enough, each person walked to TJ and gave him a hug and said something nice to him like, "I missed you today, "I hope you get feeling better, We'll have to get together some time."

Those same phrases were repeated over and until TJ was sick of listening to them. Grandma promised to bring him a tray of cookies. Grandpa promised to take him to the car race next time it was in town. Uncle Pete said I could bring a few of my friends and have lunch at his and Aunt Mary's restaurant. It's amazing how they all wanted to do something for Tommy. They hardly knew he was around before.

CHAPTER
SEVEN

TJ was doing very well. He worked all summer and saved a good amount of cash.

Many Elite colleges were vying for his attendance. They offered him everything the great schools could.

He ended going to an Ivy League college that wasn't too far from home. They gave him a full scholarship and a few other perks. He figured if he could get into an Ivy League College, he would have the best coach, and he was right. Coach Andrews was the best. He was hoping to be able to be in the Olympics in two years.

He felt bad that Jackie wasn't recruited by the same college. He was going to a great college, but not with TJ.

Tom and Janet were extremely proud of TJ. He had passed all of their expectations. And besides, he wouldn't be that far from home. He would be expected to be at all family gatherings. They would send him care packages at least once a month. All of his favorite things like Twinkies, M&Ms, donut holes and lots of chocolates.

They didn't know that he was on a restricted diet. He had to stay lean and trim for his competitions. He would give all of his 'goodies' away to his dorm friends. They were thrilled.

He was asked to join a Fraternity. He thought seriously about it. He even went to a couple of meetings, but decided that wasn't for him.

He talked to a few friends he had made, and they explained all of the Hazing, Drinking, and Sex Parties. Joe said, "Hazing can be terrible. I heard that they make you get drunk and make you do all sorts of terrible and humiliating things. You are told not to tell anyone. I thought maybe I would give it a try. They kept telling me about the Prestige it would bring to me. That was one of the better Fraternities. No, thanks. I value my education too much."

"Thanks, Joe. I certainly don't need any trouble."

He told the Frat Brothers that he was on a strict diet and had to keep his girlish figure. They laughed and told him he was a Prude. He replied, "I may be a prude, but I have years ahead of me, and I don't want a bad reputation hanging over me for the rest of my life."

Actually, Joe was telling the truth. TJ found out much later that many of the men were expelled from college for "Actions Unbecoming a Student of their caliber". Ouch!

Joe became TJ's best friend. He was also on the swimming team, so they spent a lot of time together swimming, working out and studying. They were also Dorm Brothers.

TJ remembered Jackie and the good times they had spent together. He wrote to Jackie and told him what a wonderful time he was having at College. And about his good friend Joe.

Jackie wrote back and told TJ he was thinking of dropping out of college. It just wasn't what he was looking for. He would probably go to work at his father's office as a gopher. He told TJ that he was glad that he had found a good friend like Joe.

That was the last time TJ heard from Jackie. He sent several letters to Jackie's home address, but never heard from him again.

Joe didn't have the closeness that TJ had with his family. TJ became Joe's family, along with Tom and Janet.

* * * * *

TJ received a letter from home.

Dear TJ,

Thanksgiving is just around the corner and we would like very much for you to come home for the Holidays. I will be fixing the turkey and dressing that you love so much. Of course, all of our relatives will be here. I know you're not too fond of that idea, but of course, we want to show you off. I'll bet no one else in the family will have a son that is on the Swim Team of a famous Ivy League School. I don't mean to brag, but I will force myself.

Please let us know if you are able to come.

Love,
Mom

* * * * *

"Joe, I just received a letter from my Mom. She asked me to come home for Thanksgiving Dinner," TJ announced.

"I would like you to come with me."

"Sorry, I'm not into family get-togethers with a family I don't know," Joe stated.

"Then I will write to my Mom and tell her I won't be there."

Joe panicked, "No, you can't do that. They are looking forward to seeing you," Joe said.

"Sorry, I don't go without you. If you don't go, I don't go," TJ grinned a big smile.

"You don't even know if I would be asked," Joe said.

"I will let them know that if I can't bring you, I will stay in the dorm with you."

Joe sighed a big sigh, "Okay, if they will allow me to grace their presence, I will go with you."

"They are good people, Joe. They would treat you as their own Son."

"Good Grief, another son like you? I don't know how they would react to someone like me."

"What's wrong with you? Did you forget to tell me something?"

"No, Silly. I'm not just your Everyday Joe."

"There's no doubt about it, you are a different species," TJ admitted.

* * * * *

A week later, TJ received another letter from Mom:

> Dear TJ,
>
> We would be thrilled for you to bring your friend, Joe.
>
> Whenever your break ends, we will look forward to seeing you and meeting Joe. Any friend of yours is a Son of ours. We look forward to seeing both of you.
>
> Love,
> Mom

* * * * *

TJ read the letter from Mom to Joe. "I knew you would be welcome. I have great parents. You will love them."

"I don't know. Maybe it will be fine, but I don't know," Joe said. "Maybe my parents will want me to have Thanksgiving with them."

"Why don't you check with them? I would really like you to come to my house. If you don't go with me, I think I will stay here at the dorm and eat a salad."

Joe looked surprised, "I wouldn't want you to do that. There's nothing like a homemade Thanksgiving Dinner with all the trimmings."

"Yes, but I get totally bored. I feel out of place in my own home. There will be about fifty relatives there. I have about as much in common with them as the Man in the Moon."

Joe gave in, "I'll get in touch with my parents. If they want me to come home, maybe you could come with me."

"That way, we will be together on Thanksgiving," TJ interjected.

* * * * *

Joe heard from his parents about a week later.

He read the letter to TJ.

> Dear Joe,
>
> We would love to have you and your friend here for Thanksgiving Dinner. However, we will be flying to the Hamptons to be with John and Gloria. I'm sorry we can't have Dinner at home.
>
> I hope you have a good dinner in the school cafeteria or maybe a nice restaurant. See you soon.
>
> Love,
> Mom and Dad

Joe folded the letter and threw it in the trash. "See, I told you they wouldn't want me to come home for Thanksgiving."

TJ got a big grin on his face, "I guess that takes care of Thanksgiving. We'll spend it with my family. Maybe Christmas we can spend with your family. That way we will get to know both families."

Joe came back with, "We can give it a try."

TJ wrote to his parents and let them know that he and Joe would be home for Thanksgiving."

* * * * *

TJ always seemed to be a person who would rather be alone. He did a lot of thinking. Sometimes his thoughts would be what his vocation would be. He was taking a couple of serious classes that might lead to a career later. He couldn't be a professional swimmer for too long. He probably could stay with his swimming until he was in his mid-thirties at the latest. He loved swimming, however, he had to be practical too. He was taking Political Science.

* * * * *

TJ wasn't able to sleep. His mind was running in circles. What is the next step in his career? He didn't want to wait to find out when he wanted to complete his education. He felt he had to decide what academic classes he had to take to complete his education.'

"Joe, are you awake?"

Joe just hummed, indication that he had been deep in sleep.

"Joe, wake up. We need to talk."

"We can talk in the morning if it is that important," Joe remarked.

"No, Joe, I want to talk now, while my mind is fresh," TJ said.

"Well, my mind isn't fresh. I just want to finish my sleep," Joe insisted.

TJ got out of the lower bunk bed and stood and shook Joe, "Come on. I need to talk".

"This is ridiculous. I see no reason to wake a sleeping person just because you need to talk. I don't." Joe turned over and proceeded to return to his sleep.

"I would talk to you if you couldn't sleep."

"Okay, you have my attention. What is so urgent?" Joe was frustrated and tired.

"I've been thinking; when my swimming career is finished, what am I going to do?"

"You woke me up for that?" Joe was getting irritated.

"Well, you are my best friend. I don't know who else to talk to."

"I won't be your best friend very long, if I don't get my sleep," Joe said.

"I think this is very important. I won't be able to swim forever. After I have a couple of Olympics under my belt, I might be done."

"Don't be silly. You will still be young enough to do something with your life. You will probably get married and raise children. That's what all parents wait for. They want grandchildren to spoil." Joe turned toward the wall, "Now leave me alone so I can get back to sleep."

TJ was quiet after that. Joe was right. They both needed sleep.

* * * * *

When Joe woke up, TJ was up and ready for his morning swim. Noticing Joe, TJ said, "I'm sorry I woke you up last night. Sometimes I get carried away with my thoughts."

"I'm sorry I was so grouchy. I get that way sometimes if I get woken up before I am ready," Joe said apologetically.

TJ tried to redeem himself, "When I get something on my mind and it seems so important to me, I have to talk it out."

"Seriously, are you taking any major classes that you will be able to fall back on when you are finished with swimming?"

"Why would I want to do anything else? Swimming is my life, Joe answered.

"What if you are injured or feel like you want to quit. What would you do?"

"Nothing is going to happen. I'm satisfied with my life."

"Well, what if you decided to get married and have a family? What kind of work would you have to do?" TJ was serious.

"I don't know. I haven't given it any thought. I can't see me doing anything else besides swimming. Why all of this right now?" Joe asked.

"I just know there has to be more to life than this." TJ said.

"What kind of vocation are you thinking about?" Joe queried.

"Well, there is a lot that can be done in Physical Science," TJ replied.

"Such as?"

"Arts, Technical Education, Civics, Health, Literacy and a number of others."

"They sound boring to me. I'm only interested in Swimming." Joe turned and walked out the door.

TJ hurried behind him. "You only care about Swimming?"

"There's nothing else. I have to keep up my academics, but there is nothing there I would want to spend my life doing," Joe said.

"That's sad. There has to be more. I just don't feel like I can keep going without another goal in mind," TJ rebutted.

CHAPTER
EIGHT

The wind was blowing fiercely. Winter could be just around the corner. TJ thought he could feel snow. He looked around and saw nothing except his best friend Joe.

As they were nearing TJ's parent's house, it looked strange. It didn't look like home anymore.

"I hope Thanksgiving won't be too bad for you. I find it extremely boring," TJ lamented.

"I'm sure it will be fine. I'm looking forward to meeting your Mom and Dad." Joe smiled and spoke sincerely.

"They are great people. I couldn't ask for anything better."

* * * * *

As they pulled up to the front porch, Tom and Janet appeared. Janet waved and shouted, "Hi, boys. We're so glad you decided to come. I'm sure you will have a great time."

TJ and Joe smiled at each other and waved a hearty greeting.

Tom opened the passenger door for Joe. TJ exited on his own. He was glad that his parents seemed excited to see their son and his friend.

Janet escorted the boys to TJ's room. Tom trailed behind. Upon entering the room, TJ noticed a cot set up for him to sleep on. He had wondered what they would do about sleeping arrangements for the friends.

Janet said to the boys, "I'm sure you men are tired after your trip. If you would like, you can go to bed to get a good night's sleep or you could come down and have popcorn and hot chocolate."

The two men looked at each other and grinned. "I guess that answers our question. Popcorn and hot chocolate it is." Both of them answered at once.

"We'll put a few of our things away and then come down," TJ remarked.

Joe said, "That sounds great. You have a great pair of parents. I only wish mine cared half as much."

* * * * *

They could smell the popcorn all the way upstairs. Joe said, "I am so excited. I can only imagine spending time with parents. Let's hurry!"

Five minutes later they were both in their pajamas and down stairs. The card table was set up next to the couch. A large bowl of popcorn and a pitcher of hot chocolate with bowls and cups waiting to be filled.

Tom and Janet were seated on chairs in the opposite sides of the room. As the boys were seated on the couch, Janet asked Joe, "Tell me something about you. Where are you from? What do your parents do. Why didn't you go to their house for Thanksgiving?"

Everything started to feel awkward. Joe looked at TJ who was smiling, "Well, I was born and raised in Philadelphia. The city is so big, it sometimes scares me. They told me they are going to the Hamptons for Thanksgiving. That would have left me alone. Thanks to TJ and his gracious parents, I was asked to come here."

Tom said, "We're glad to have you here. We like to meet his friends."

"We've been good friends ever since we started College. We are in the same dorm," TJ stated. "We are on the same Swim Team."

"Well, we are happy to have you both here on this occasion."

"Well, we are happy to be here." TJ beamed.

Janet said, "We were just starting a movie. Would you like to watch it with us? It's still quite early."

"We would love that," Joe said.

* * * * *

Before the movie was over, both students were sleeping. Tom nudged TJ and suggested that they retreat to the bedroom.

TJ awakened Joe and both went up the stairs. TJ let Joe sleep in his bed and he took the cot.

Sometime later, TJ felt Joe crawl beside him on the cot. Now that was awkward. TJ didn't say anything, although it was crowded. He turned toward the wall and Joe cuddled next to his friend, spoon style. TJ tried to ignore it and soon fell back to sleep. Before long he could feel Joe's hand move up and down TJ's side. For some reason TJ didn't mind. This was the closest anybody had ever slept with him.

Joe woke up in a particularly good mood. TJ was perplexed. Did Joe mean anything that had happened or was he just lonesome. He didn't know what to say or how to react.

Finally, Joe spoke, "Did you enjoy last night?"

TJ tried to overlook the incident and said, "The popcorn and the hot chocolate was unexpected and great."

"No, silly. After we went to bed," Joe smirked.

"I'm not ready to talk about it. I want to think about it for a while." TJ seemed confused. He wasn't sure how he felt. He liked to cuddle, but the rest was totally foreign to him. He hadn't felt that way before. He didn't know how he should feel. Maybe time will tell.

* * * * *

TJ could smell pumpkin pie. One of the great smells of Thanksgiving. It's time to help Mom with the dinner preparations.

"Breakfast, Boys?" Mom asked.

"Whatcha got, Mrs. Williams?"

"Lot of stuff, Joe. How did you sleep last night? I'll bet TJ was glad to be back in his own bed," Janet said.

"He let me have his bed. He slept on the cot," Joe announced.

"Well, that was nice of TJ. Of course, I wouldn't expect anything different."

"Mom, can I make the biscuits?"

Janet looked at him questionably, "Sure, if you remember how."

"It's just like riding a bike, you never forget."

Joe looked at him strangely, "You? Make biscuits?'

"Yes, I used to make them all the time when I lived at home."

"I'll wash my hands and get started. Joe, do you want to help?"

"No thank you, I'll have some pancakes and watch", was Joe's answer.

TJ proceeded to get the flour, Crisco, milk and salt out.

Joe watched TJ very intently as he ate his pancakes smothered in butter and homemade maple syrup. TJ looked like the professional chefs he had seen on tv. He was amazed.

It wasn't long before the biscuits were in the oven.

"What can I do, Mrs. Williams?" Joe questioned.

"See if you can help Mr. Williams set the tables up and get the centerpieces on each one."

Joe said, "Yes, ma'am. I'm sure I can do that."

After he had gone from the room, Janet said, "He seems like a nice boy. Have you known him long?"

"Just since the semester started. We have the same dorm room. And best of all, he is also on the swim team, so we exercise together, practice swim together, we eat lunch together, and we have a couple of classes together."

"Whew! No wonder you are such good friends," Mom acknowledged.

"Okay, what's next?" TJ said wanting to change the subject.

"What do you mean?"

"Dinner, remember? I'm helping you," TJ said.

"Well, gravy needs to be made," came the answer.

"Yes, but you make the best gravy in the world."

"You can learn. I have saved all of the drippings from the turkey. I can teach you from there. Why don't you go to Culinary School? You'll need something to do when you can no longer compete in swimming."

"It's funny you should mention that. I have been trying to think of a vocation to go into after swimming and the Olympics."

"What is Joe going to do when he is done swimming?" Mom asked.

"I've been asking him that same thing. I've gotten nowhere with that category," was TJ's excuse. "He thinks he will be swimming the rest of his life. I love swimming, too, but I am trying to be realistic. I know if I am lucky and work extremely hard, I might be able to be in swim competitions until my mid-thirties. I have to look ahead. What if I want to get married and have a family? I have to think of that."

"Do you have a girl in mind?"

"No, I really have not been interested in dating, although, I feel like I should be paying more attention to the female persuasion." TJ remembered.

"What about Joe? Does he have a girlfriend?" Mom inquired.

"I'm fairly sure he hasn't. He never talks about girls," TJ answered. He couldn't get his mind off of the episode last night.

Mom said, "I like him. He seems like a nice person with good manners."

TJ couldn't think of a good comeback. His mind was muddled.

Dinner preparations were well underway when Joe came in. The tables had all been put up with white linen tablecloths and centerpieces in the middle so the wind could not blow the tablecloths away.

People were starting to arrive with dishes to pass. Uncle Pete and Aunt Mary came with her famous Jell-O Salad. They came in the house to say 'Hello' to the ones in the kitchen. Grandpa and Grandma came in with her wonderful Apple Pie.

Uncle Pete said, "TJ it is so good to see you. Who is your friend?"

"Uncle Pete, this is Joe. He is my friend and Dorm Companion, and Swim partner." They cordially shook hands and exchanged smiles.

About that time Grandpa said, "I'm glad you were able to come.

Hello Joe, we are TJ's grandparents. It's good to meet you and to have you here for Thanksgiving. We have a lot to be thankful for."

"Yes, Sir we have," Joe returned as he shook Grandpas hand briskly.

Next Aunt Ellen came in with her cranberry sauce. She looked dubiously at Joe, "Who is this fine looking young man?"

TJ introduced the two of them when Uncle Harold entered. "This must be Joe. Grandpa was saying what a nice young man his is." He grabbed for Joe's hand before he was able to extend it.

Uncle Fred was the next one to enter the kitchen. Uncle Fred carried the Green Bean casserole and handed it to TJ. Aunt Anita said her hellos while hugging each person, including Joe, before they could be introduced. "You should go outside and introduce him to Greg and his new wife Alta.

It was really a pleasure to have a change of scenery and fresh air.

It seemed like there were more cousins than TJ could remember. They were already engaged in touch football. Greg yelled to TJ, "Wouldn't you and your friend like to play touch football with us? We could use a couple more players."

"I'll come and play with you," said Joe, "Come on TJ, this could be fun."

"Nah, you go, I'll watch from the porch," as TJ denied the offer.

* * * * *

"Dinner's on. Come and eat. Children first, then teens and last of all the Adults. Grandpa and Grandma can go first of the adults."

"Mom made a great announcer." TJ said in his proudest voice.

"I think your whole family is great."

"Yeah, they are pretty great," TJ had to agree.

"Let's get the kitchen cleaned up and go for a walk," Joe suggested.

"Okay, the family usually takes a nap after dinner, anyway," TJ returned.

"Perfect, maybe we can get some things straightened out," Joe added.

* * * * *

Joe and TJ started walking toward the barn. Some of the children were playing tag outside. Almost all of the adults were napping in front of the television. They call it watching the football game. It's funny how no one remembers many of the plays.

When they neared the barn, suddenly Joe grabbed for TJ's hand. "This is awkward. I just don't get holding hands with a man," TJ mentioned.

Joe said, "Why? Don't you feel any attraction between us? I love you."

TJ looked shocked, "What? What are you saying? I like you. We are best buds. You love me?"

Joe retaliated, "You invited me here for Thanksgiving; I assumed it was because you felt about me the same way I feel about you."

"I knew we were friends. I invited you because you didn't have anywhere to go. And I didn't feel like coming home at all. But maybe if I had a friend to come with me it wouldn't be so bad, but I didn't expect this. I like you, but I am not 'in love' with you."

They didn't say anything else for a long time. They followed the fence along the road for quite a while. Then they started back toward the house.

Finally, Joe made the statement, "I want to go back to the Dorm. I can see this is not going to work out."

"Couldn't we wait until tomorrow?" TJ asked. "It may look funny if we leave so soon."

"I'd like to leave right away. I'm embarrassed. I thought you felt the same way I do."

TJ tried to smooth things. "Let's wait until tomorrow to leave. Then maybe it won't look like we have had a problem."

"Please, TJ, let's leave as soon as possible and return back to the Dorm. Tell your parents anything you want, but I want to get back to my own space."

"Ok, but this won't be easy."

* * * * *

TJ found his mother in the kitchen cutting the pies into even pieces. "I don't know how you do that with such precision."

Janet was startled, "Sorry, I didn't hear you come in. Where's Joe?"

"He went upstairs to pack. We're going back to the Dorm," was the honest reply.

"I'm sorry. I thought the two of you were having a good time. It seemed so good to see you enjoying yourselves." She turned and looked at the pies once again. "Did we do something wrong?"

"No, Mom, he was feeling out of place. I have such wonderful parents and his went away for the weekend and didn't even invite him to go. I felt obligated to invite him to our house." He looked at the floor, "It just didn't work out."

"Maybe, we could take a couple of pieces of pie with us. I love you, Mom."

"And I, you."

"I know and I am so grateful that I have you and Dad to come to. I feel sorry for Joe. He hasn't anybody."

Mom blushed, "What kind of pie would you like to take with you?"

"I think Apple Pie sounds great." TJ turned and walked toward the stairs. He stopped by his dad to watch the game for just a minute. He just wanted to feel the closeness with his dad that he hadn't felt for a long time.

Then he headed up the stairs to his bedroom. Joe was all packed and was laying on the bed looking upward. He didn't say anything.

TJ started packing his things. He was sad that things had turned out the way they had. He enjoyed having Joe as his best friend. He never dreamed things would be so awkward and meaningless. Sometimes he wishes he had not felt so different from other people.

* * * * *

"Mom, we're heading back to the School. Thank you for everything and for accepting Joe like he was part of the family. It means a lot to me that I am able to bring my friends home and that they will be welcome," TJ explained.

"I'm sorry you couldn't stay longer. It's a long ride back to the College. You could wait till morning," his Mom said.

"Joe has a paper that he has to present to the Professor Monday and he hasn't started it yet. He thought he would have plenty of time. He thinks if he has a good night's sleep, his mind will be fresh and clear."

About that time, Joe came down stairs with his suitcase. He told everyone good-bye and thanked them for their hospitality. He hugged Janet, "Everyone has been so nice to me. You have really made me feel at home. You are wonderful parents. I wish my parents thought as much of me."

"I'm sure they will be happy to see you at Christmas," Janet said.

"I doubt that, but I'm used to being alone on holidays," Joe whispered.

"TJ, I'm ready when you are," was Joe's next remark.

TJ said his good-byes to everyone and especially thanked his Mom and Dad for their cordiality toward Joe.

Joe and TJ waved as they departed out of the driveway.

CHAPTER
NINE

The ride back was quiet. No one said anything. It was snowing, so the roads were a little slippery. Both men had a lot on their minds. TJ was wondering if he could swim tomorrow morning. Would the Gym be open, or would it be closed because of the holiday.

Joe was thinking about moving to another Dorm Room. Is there an opening? Would the man be as easy to get along with as TJ? He was sorry that he came on to TJ as he did. They had been such good friends, that he thought TJ would be ready for the next step. Apparently, he had misjudged TJ.

* * * * *

The guys took their luggage from the car to their third floor apartment.

Joe said, "I'm gonna see if I can get into another apartment."

"Why? We usually get along so good," TJ stated.

"We don't want the same thing," was Joe's reply.

"We both are on the swim team and we have some classes together. What is the problem?" TJ asked.

"I think that's obvious," Joe said.

"Okay, so we had a misunderstanding," said TJ.

"More like a miscommunication."

"Probably, why can't we remain friends?" TJ queried.

"Because I want more. I don't think I could stay here and see you every day and every night and be objective. I told you I love you, but you don't feel the same," Joe declared.

TJ whispered, "Do what you think is best."

* * * * *

Joe made many enquiries before he received the answer he wanted.

He informed TJ, "I will be moving down the hall tomorrow. This guy might be just what I need and want."

"Good luck, Joe, I wish you all the best."

Joe moved to apartment 4. TJ stayed in number 9. TJ didn't get a roommate for a while. He rather liked being alone. He was able to do what he wanted, when he wanted.

* * * * *

Christmas had just passed. Mom and Dad were sad because TJ didn't come home. He explained that Joe had moved to another apartment and he was alone. He wasn't in any mood to see family, any family.

TJ saw Joe at practice and at meets. They had nothing to say to each other. That was enough to last him. Joe seemed to be contented in his new environment.

TJ was okay with not having a roommate. Actually, he felt he had more time to study and practice swimming. His favorite time was midnight. There usually weren't many men there swimming. He swam hard for about an hour, then he would go back to his Dorm room. After all of the strenuous exercise there was no way he could go to sleep, so he studied for about another hour until his eyes wouldn't focus anymore.

He felt he was getting along very well. His grades were exemplar and his swimming was improving every day or night as the case may be.

His coach kept pushing him to work harder and learn strokes he didn't have quite right. He enjoyed the way he was stressing himself to be better. He really felt he was accomplishing his goals.

He wanted to write letters to his mom at least once a week. That didn't always work out because he was so busy. TJ still received 'care' packages once a month. But NO sweets. She sent a lot of a variety of nuts and granola bars (homemade of course). He enjoyed them so much. He would limit his goodies to one granola bar in the morning and a small handful of nuts in the evening.

TJ also was becoming quite the chef. He made his own meals and fixed some kind of yummy desert to share with the other men on that floor. As soon as this year of classes is over, he would sign up for Culinary School. Except for swimming. He HAD to continue that course. Going to the Olympics was still his dream.

* * * * *

During the last semester of School TJ met a girl. She was different. She reminded him of his mother. Not in looks or size. She loved to cook and baking was her specialty. Her name was Angelica. To him, she was an angel, halo and all.

He met her in the lunchroom. She sat down by TJ and said, "This food, I use that loosely, is terrible. Doesn't anyone know how to make a ham and cheese sandwich?"

TJ laughed, "I doubt it. My name is Tom, but because my father's name is Tom, I got stuck with TJ. I really don't mind."

"My name is Angelica, but believe me, I am NO angel."

"I'm glad to meet you. Do you come here often?"

"Often enough to see a good looking man, sitting by himself, half eating his sandwich."

"Believe me, after this semester, I am enrolling in Culinary School." TJ had never met a girl like Angelica.

"Really! I have already signed up for it. You know, it's quite pricy."

"I had heard that," TJ replied. "I have been in the kitchen with my mother ever since I was an itty-bitty child."

Angelica came back with, "I wasn't so lucky. My mother was a lousy cook. She couldn't even boil water without burning it. I decided I was going to learn to cook or starve."

"You're exaggerating a little bit, aren't you?"

"Not at all," Angelica said.

"You have to meet my mother. You would love her," TJ assumed.

"I just met you, and already I want to ask you if you would like to go to the Coffee Shop for a refreshment after your last class?"

"I don't drink coffee, but maybe they have something I could drink," Angelica decided.

"You don't drink coffee?" TJ replied as he raised one eyebrow.

"No, I'm a Mormon. We don't drink coffee." She answered.

"What is a Mormon? I have never heard of them." TJ looked suspicious.

"We are a religion. We have strict rules about what we drink."

"Is that anything like the Shakers or Seventh Day Adventists?"

"No, we are different," She said as she raised one eyebrow to tease TJ.

"Well, we need to get to our next class. Let's meet here right at 3:00."

"Yes, let's, this should be interesting."

His thoughts exactly.

They went in opposite directions. All the time he was thinking, what is a Mormon? I know it is a religion, but what makes them different? She looks normal. I'll have to ask some questions.

* * * * *

He arrived at his English Theory class early. A man named Richard sat down next to him. TJ felt foolish, but decided to strike up a conversation.

"Do you know anything about a religion called Mormon?"

Richard answered, "All I know is that they are weird. The men have many wives and they wear strange clothes and they don't drink coffee, tea, or any form of alcohol."

"What do they do for entertainment?" TJ wondered.

"I don't know, but I would stay away from them, if I were you. They might try to convert you." Richard looked serious.

TJ returned, "I can take care of myself."

Richard looked at TJ as if he were from outer space.

* * * * *

Three o'clock sharp TJ was at the appointed place. Angelica was already there. She looked beautiful. She didn't look strange or wear different clothes.

"Hi, shall we go?" TJ asked as he put his hand on her back to guide her.

"Can I ask you a question?"

Angelica nodded.

"How many mothers do you have?" He was feeling a little foolish.

"Ah, I see you have been asking questions about Mormons."

It was his turn to nod.

"I have one mother and one father and three brothers and one sister." Angelica looked suspicious, waiting for the next question.

"I'm sorry," TJ related, "I was just curious, because I had never heard of that religion before."

"If you have any more questions, I would be happy to answer them if I can."

As they arrived at the Coffee Shop, TJ held the door for her and they entered.

They both looked at the menu board contemplating what they should order.

Angelica decided first, "I'll have a chocolate milk shake with whipped cream on top."

"That sounds great, I'll have the same." TJ ordered for both of them, then they found an empty table and made their way to it. TJ held out the chair for his companion.

Angelica remarked emphatically, "You have been taught well. You are quite the gentleman."

TJ blushed. He had been taught at a young age how to treat women. He just said, "Thank you."

A guy brought the milk shakes to the table. "Those are huge. I've never had milk shakes that big."

Someone across the room yelled, "Hi Angelica. How are you doing?

She smiled and waved a hello.

"A friend of yours?" TJ asked.

"Yes, he is in one of my classes," Angelica remembered.

"How would you like to tell me a little about your religion?" TJ inquired.

"Sure," was the answer.

The more he spoke to her, the more he was curious about her.

"If you would like, you could come to my Dorm room about 4:00 tomorrow. I'll have dinner ready. You do like spaghetti, don't you?"

"Of course. Which Dorm is yours?"

"Number 3. I'm on the second floor number 205. When you enter the building, you will have to speak with my Dorm Mother. She will call up to my room. Then you go up the stairs. Turn left. My room is the second on the left. The door will be open."

"I hope I can remember all that. I'll be there."

"All you have to remember is Dorm building number 3. Then speak to my Dorm Mother for directions. I'm the only Angelica in the building. It's impossible to get lost. Everyone knows where I am."

* * * * *

Dear Mom,

I've met a girl. She's wonderful, beautiful, loves to cook, and reminds me of you. She's great. I can't wait for you and Dad to meet her.

Love,
TJ

TJ couldn't wait to get this letter sent to his parents. This would be a surprise, because he hardly ever writes letters.

The day came for the spaghetti dinner. He could hardly get there fast enough.

He was looking around for Dorm 3. He went up and down the road. Where is it? There's only one place he hadn't looked. He found Dorm 2, so he looked behind it. There it was, all the time. Three minutes to four. I'll never make it on time. This is a very bad first impression. Well, almost first.

He had a hard time finding a parking place. He rushed to the front door.

There was the Dorm Mother. She took one look at me and pointed to the staircase. I must have looked a fright. I didn't have a chance to introduce myself or ask for directions.

I ran, yes ran, up the stairs and made a quick left.

I could smell spaghetti as soon as I got to the top of the stairs. Wow! Could she cook! It has to be love at first bite.

The door was open, as she said it would be. I stopped and knocked on the door casing.

Right there in front of my eyes was the most beautiful girl I had ever seen.

"Come in silly. I've been waiting for you."

I could think of many reasons why I was late, but nothing recognizable came out of my mouth. All I could say was, "I'm sorry."

I looked at the wonderfully set table and there were place settings for four.

"Are others coming?" I asked.

"Yes," she said, "The Sister Missionaries. They should be here any time."

TJ looked disappointed, "Sister Missionaries?"

"You wanted to know more about my church, so I invited them to eat with us."

"Oh, I thought we could have a cozy little dinner, just the two of us."

"I'm sorry you got that impression. They won't stay too long. Would you like some lemonade while we wait?"

"Wow! I've never been asked that before," TJ said. "Sure, I'll have some lemonade."

Angelica retreated to the refrigerator in the kitchenette. She soon returned with the refreshment.

TJ related, "This is the best lemonade I have ever tasted. Not too sour, and not too sweet. Just right with lots of ice to keep it cool."

Soon there was a knock on the doorpost. "Come in, Sisters. This is the gentleman I was telling you about. Sister Carter and Sister Smith, I'd like you to meet TJ Williams."

TJ stood and reached for each hand as the women reached for his.

"Are you really sisters? You have different last names."

Sister Carter revealed, "We are all brothers and sisters in the church."

"That makes it convenient if you forget someone's first name," TJ jokingly stated.

Everyone laughed and TJ started feeling more at ease.

"The food is ready, let's eat."

They all retreated to the table. Angelica asked, "Sister Smith, would you offer the blessing?"

The three women bowed their heads, so TJ thought he had better reciprocate and did the same.

Sister Smith said the prayer and blessed all of the people she was able to think of.

"That was a lovely prayer. I've never heard one like that before," was TJ's assessment.

"Thank you. What church do you belong to?"

Looking a little sheepish and embarrassed, he answered, "I have never been to church. My parents don't belong to any church. I guess they didn't think it was necessary."

"Angelica, this spaghetti is the best I have ever had. And who would have thought to have a green salad with it? Did you make the garlic rolls?" TJ stated, trying to redeem himself.

"A garden salad and garlic rolls are traditional. I'm glad you are enjoying them."

TJ said, "I definitely am. My mother is a great cook, but I don't think she ever made spaghetti this good. You'll have to come to my house and make it for my Mom and Dad."

"Do you have any brothers and sisters?" Sister Smith asked.

"None, I am an only child."

Angelica said, "I would love to make a spaghetti dinner for them if they wouldn't be offended."

"I don't think they would be offended. I think they would love to learn a new technique," TJ responded.

After the dinner was over, the Mormon Missionaries told a few facts about their church. They didn't want to overwhelm TJ the first time he had met them.

By 6:30 they left to go to another home to teach the Gospel. Sister Carter asked if she could give a prayer.

Angelica stated, "That would be great".

After that, they both shook hands with Angelica and TJ. Then said goodnight and left.

"Those Sisters were very nice," TJ remarked.

TJ and Angelica settled down to watch a little tv, after the dishes had been done and put away.

Angelica's roommate came in about 9:00. Angelica introduced her to him.

TJ got the hint that it was time for him to go back to his own room.

"Angelica, I had a terrific time. The food was magnificent and the Sisters were nice and had great senses of humor. Hopefully, I will see you tomorrow."

He wondered if he could give her a little kiss. Maybe that wouldn't be appropriate. Maybe next time.

* * * * *

TJ received a letter from his mother.

> Dear TJ,
>
> We are so excited to hear that you have met a girl you are interested in. I hope you will bring her home soon so we can meet her. I'm not sure I want her to fix supper. My kitchen has always been my domain. Let us know when you will bring her home.
>
> Love,
> Mom

This wasn't the only letter he had received from his Mom. Others that were sent were about what was going on at the farm. That last letter was the only one concerning Angelica.

* * * * *

TJ and Angelica went on a few dates. They went to the movies, bowling, tennis and went to a Minor League Baseball game. She was great to be around. She is so much like his mom.

Angelica again invited TJ over to her dorm room for Pizza. She invited the sisters over too. She had the pizza delivered. They ate off of paper plates so there were no dishes to wash. That made it nice. Washing dishes was not one of his favorite things to do.

After the pizza was almost gone, the Sisters started telling TJ about the Book of Mormon. TJ listened politely. He didn't understand much. At

Nine o'clock sharp, the Sister Missionaries made a hasty exit. At last TJ and Angelica were alone.

"Angelica, my parents would like to meet you. I told them what a good cook you are, and maybe we could persuade you to fix a spaghetti dinner for them. If this weekend is good, we could shop for everything you would need for the preparation."

"Maybe your mother wouldn't want another woman in her kitchen", was Angelica's rebuttal.

"When my mother gets to know you, she will love you as much as I do," TJ admitted.

The girl looked at him strangely. Love had never been brought up before.

"You love me?" Angelica asked. "We never had discussed that possibility."

"I figured you knew. I have never felt this way about a woman before. Of course, I love you and I hope you feel the same about me."

Angelica was dumbfounded. She didn't know what to say. "I would be happy to fix dinner for your parents. If you don't mind, I would like to get the food on the way there. I don't want to put them out."

"That can be arranged," he said with a big sheepish grin.

* * * * *

Friday night they stopped at the Super Market and bought all that was needed for a gourmet meal.

Angelica said, "We better stop at McDonalds and get a couple of burgers. It will be too late to fix a big meal by the time we get there."

"You think of everything. You are amazing."

"Will your parents have room enough for me to stay overnight?"

"Yes, we have a big farm house. There is plenty of room."

"You never told me about the farm." "

That will give us something to talk about while driving," TJ said.

Explaining how a farm runs took quite a while. Actually, he was glad when they arrived. He was tired of explaining how to milk cows, and gather eggs from the yard.

Angelica was excited. She had never been on a farm before.

* * * * *

TJ parked the car and walked around to the other side and held the door open for Angelica. Then he picked the bag of groceries up. He held the girl's elbow and guided her to the house.

TJ's dad opened the door just as the couple reached it.

"Dad this is Angelica, this is my father Tom."

"Come in", Tom insisted.

"I'm glad to meet you, Tom," she said as she held out her hand for him to shake.

He thought that was strange, but he didn't want her to misunderstand, so he shook her hand lightly.

She took hold of his hand and said, "No, this is the way to shake hands," She gave his hand a firm shake and smiled at him.

He smiled back and invited her to enter the foyer. Tom led her to the kitchen where, of course, Janet was. She was cleaning the stove, where something she was cooking earlier had spilled over.

TJ announced, "This is Angelica. This is my mother Janet."

Angelica held out her hand to Janet. TJ's mom wondered what she was supposed to do.

TJ took his mother's hand and put it in Angelica's. The girl gave a strong shake and smiled. Janet smiled in return.

"I'm just about done here, why don't I make some popcorn and retreat to the living room and get acquainted."

Angelica said, "I would like that very much".

Janet proceeded to put a bag of popcorn in a pan that she kept especially for making popcorn. A couple of minutes later it started to pop. Janet shook the pan until it didn't pop anymore. Then she put a little salt and butter on it. Perfectly made popcorn.

"Would you like something to drink? I have some fresh coffee made", Janet stated.

"Water would be fine," Angelica relayed, being polite.

"Where would you like me to sleep tonight, Mrs. Williams?"

* * * * *

It seemed like they talked for hours. Getting to know each other takes time. After about an hour, Angelica said, "I think I'm getting sleepy."

Janet said, "We have a room all set up for you. TJ, show Angelica to Uncle Billy's room."

"You mean the haunted room?"

"TJ, that isn't very nice."

"Oh, I forgot. We're not supposed to mention that, are we?"

"I'm sure I'll sleep just fine if Uncle Billy doesn't mind," Angelica smiled as she went along with the joke.

TJ picked her bag up and led the way to Uncle Billy's room.

"I think Uncle Billy has a very nice room. I'm sure he and I will get along very well."

TJ leaned forward to give her a goodnight kiss, but she said goodnight and shut the door.

* * * * *

When Angelica woke up, she heard the back door shut. She immediately got up and got dressed. She was hoping to be able to go with Tom, to see what he does. Never having been on a farm before, she wanted to see everything.

As she entered the kitchen, she saw a nicely set table. There was a plate, fork and knife on a freshly laundered napkin. Above those were a coffee cup and a small glass of orange juice.

She drank the juice and turned the coffee cup over on the saucer.

About that time, TJ came walking in.

Angelica said, "Do you think Tom would mind if I walked behind him and watched him?"

"No, I think he would be delighted," Janet beamed.

* * * * *

Janet fixed a hearty breakfast. Pancakes, sausage, scrambled eggs and lots of toast with jelly.

Angelica had never seen so much food at one time. She ate her fill.

"People who work on farms, whether dairy or vegetables, it doesn't matter. They are all hard workers and must sustain themselves," Janet acknowledged.

Tom said, "I'm ready to go. Are you ready, Angelica?"

She wiped her mouth after drinking the last of her orange juice, "I'm ready too," she said enthusiastically. She pushed herself away from the table and scurried to be on Tom's heels as they went out the door.

They could be seen hurrying toward the big red barn, while TJ and his mother cleared the table and started washing the dishes. Janet washed and TJ dried. It reminded him of his earlier years helping his mother.

* * * * *

Tom and Angelica went downstairs to where the cows had been resting. Tom got a big bucket of soapy water. He handed a clean rag to Angelica and motioned for her to start washing the teats. She asked, "Why do you have to wash the teats before the machines are hooked up?"

Tom explained, "They have to be clean so no foreign matter gets into the fresh milk. After the cows are milked, a big truck with a big tank on the back, put the milk in the tank and take it right off to the processing plant to be homogenized and pasteurized and put into gallon containers to be sent to stores. Other items are made out of milk too, of course. Cheese, ice cream, cream cheese, and lots of other items."

"Fascinating," Angelica mused. "What else is made of milk?"

"Of course," Tom said, "Cottage cheese, coffee cream, and cream to be whipped and made into desserts. There are dozens of food products our milk is made into."

"Fascinating," Angelica repeated.

From there they cleaned up some of the barn after the cows were herded outside. They didn't clean much, because the farm hands would do that.

"The barn must be kept spotless or the trucks will stop picking up our milk."

Angelica followed Tom outside where hay was put down for some of the cows to eat.

Then they got in Tom's pick-up truck and went where there were other trucks spreading food for the remaining cows and bulls and calves.

Angelica thought it was interesting that the cows and bulls would be following the feed trucks to be sure they got their share.

From there Tom took her where the calves were getting shots to be sure they stayed healthy. Then they had to be branded with the farm's special brand that no other farm could use.

By this time it was lunch time, so the duo went back to the house.

TJ and Janet had made some Minestrone soup.

"I knew this is a hearty soup, for all of us hard workers," Angelica laughed.

"Don't anyone laugh, Angelica did a tremendous job of helping this morning," Tom stated.

"I learned more than you'll ever know. I learned that running a dairy farm is not child's play. IT'S HARD WORK." Angelica admitted.

Tom suggested, "Maybe you would like to go out with me this afternoon as well."

"I would love to, but I would like to stay here and start the spaghetti sauce. You do want it to be ready when you come in for supper?" came the reply.

Tom got a pouty look on his face then said with a loud sigh, "Well, I guess you will just have to come back so I can show you the rest."

Angelica grinned and said in a teasing manner, "We'll see."

* * * * *

Soon, Tom had finished his soup and crackers and was off to do his chores.

Angelica asked Janet where she kept the utensils and pots she would need.

Janet led her to the very neat drawers and cupboards where she could find everything she needed.

Then the girl found all of the groceries she and TJ had brought the night before. She organized all of the meat and onions, and green peppers in one place. Then she organized all of the spices she would need in a neat row.

She went to the sink and turned the hot water on and proceeded to vigorously, washed her hands. Janet handed her a hand towel so she could dry them.

Next, Angelica heated the pot she would use to sauté the meat and vegetables until they were ready for the rest of the ingredients.

When the mixture was simmering, she washed and put away any utensils she would not need again. She put the spices back in the bag she brought from the store, so she wouldn't forget to take them home with her.

She let the mixture simmer on low for about two hours.

During this time, Janet and her guest had time to get to know each other better.

"TJ is very proud of you and Tom. He talks about you all the time. It isn't easy for him to talk about you, especially. He told me how he used to help you in the kitchen and with cleaning chores, which gave him the love of culinary work. I know he will do well in Culinary next semester."

"We are both taking at least one semester of the Culinary Course, then I will go on to an advanced class. I don't know if TJ is planning on the advanced class. Baking is also another alternative. I want to take that also."

"You are a very interesting girl. Please tell me about your family."

"Well, I come from a relatively large one. There six children and I am in the middle. My parents are very strict but also very loving."

"Excuse me, while I go and check on my sauce." She gave the mixture a good stirring to be sure it wasn't sticking on the bottom. All was well. She returned to her conversation with Janet.

"My father is a CPA and my mother is a stay-at-home mom. Believe me, my mother works every bit as hard as my dad. Taking care of six children IS a full time job."

"Please, tell me about your brothers and sisters," Janet inquired.

"Matthew is married and has a baby on the way. Mark is second. He is on a Mission for our church in Ireland.

"How long will he be in Ireland", Janet asked.

Angelica answered, "Two years. I'm number 3. Joseph is next. He is in high school. Lucas is still in grade school. Joanna is in the third grade. Well that's all of us."

"Whew, that's a group. Your parents have their hands full."

"True, especially my dad. He's the Bishop of our congregation. He is responsible for everybody within our boundaries."

Janet was puzzled. "I don't understand. What are your boundaries?"

"I'll try to explain it as simply as I can. We live in what are called Wards. I think that is like some people live in a parish. The Ward we live within is overseen by a Bishop. Some Wards are encompassed by a few blocks, whereas, some Wards encompass miles. Nevertheless, the Bishop is responsible for the welfare of everyone within his Ward, whether members of our church or not."

"Ah, I see. No wonder your father is so busy. Does he get paid to be a Bishop?" Janet asked.

"No, he works as a CPA. That is his vocation, but he is always on call if he is needed as a Bishop. So you see, he is our father, a CPA, and a Bishop."

"Excuse me, I will be right back. I need to stir the spaghetti sauce again," Angelica expressed.

She soon returned. The spaghetti sauce was coming along fine.

Janet showed interest, "What is the name of your church?"

"The Church of Jesus Christ of Latter-day Saints. It's easier to call us Mormons," the girl answered with pride.

Janet said, "I have never heard of that, but I find it very interesting."

"Do you belong to a church?" Angelica asked.

"Not really. We attend services on Easter and Christmas Eve at a church about a mile away," was the reply.

"I'm sure it won't be long before the men will be back for a hardy supper," Angelica noted. "I still have a salad to make and garlic bread to toast in the oven."

"I would be happy to help you," Janet admitted.

Angelica looked at the woman with a big grin, "I would like that. It has been so enjoyable talking to you this afternoon."

"I've enjoyed it too," Janet said with a smile.

* * * * *

"Everything is ready for the salad, if you would like to put it together. I also brought a dressing I hope you will like. I made it last night and let it stand overnight in the fridge."

Angelica turned on the oven at 425 to warm up for the garlic bread.

The guest got a large pot and put hot water in it with a good amount of salt.

Then she set the table to the best of her ability with what she had at her disposal.

When Janet had finished the salad, she put the finishing touches on the table.

About this time, the men came in from the afternoons work.

Tom aggressively asked, "When is supper ready? I'm starving."

TJ remarked, "Yeah, he worked my fingers to the bone. Did you have a nice afternoon?"

Janet piped up, "Angelica was telling me about her church. It was very fascinating.

The women put the spaghetti in a bowl, and the sauce in another. The salad was dressed with the homemade dressing, and the garlic bread was stacked on a plate.

Everyone except Angelica started to dig in. Then the girl surprised everyone by offering to bless the food.

The shock on the faces was very noticeable. "Of course, we would love to have you bless the food," Janet said.

The prayer was beautiful, blessing the food and the hands that prepared it, blessing TJ's family and farm, and thanking Heavenly Father for the lovely weekend and hospitality, and asking for a safe trip back to the College.

They would be leaving first thing in the morning.

The family was amazed. They all fell in love with Angelica. She was warm, intelligent, and beautiful. They figured she would make a wonderful addition to the family.

Oh, and the food was delicious. She had used spices Janet had never heard of. Everyone ate until they could eat no more.

* * * * *

When Angelica and TJ were ready to leave, Tom and Janet took turns hugging the girl and inviting her back.

She had made a very good first impression.

On the way to the college, the two of them talked about their weekend and how much TJ's parents liked Angelica. The conversation was light and both were happy.

TJ helped Angelica to her Dorm room. He gave her a quick kiss on her cheek and went on his way.

Back at his Dorm all he could think of was his beautiful companion. He knew he was in love, his first love.

The next day he saw her at lunch. She asked him over for dinner. He said he would be there. Would the Missionaries be there?

She said, "Of course, I try to have dinner for them at least once a week."

TJ stated, "I would like to have dinner with you alone."

"Maybe later this week," the girl related.

"Maybe I'll skip dinner tonight and come over later this week," TJ said.

"Don't you like the Missionaries?" Angelica asked.

"They are okay, I would like to be with you, without talking about the church. I'm not really interested. I really don't want to go to church and live in such a strict way," TJ answered.

"Oh, I'm so sorry to hear that. The church is a big part of my life and always will be. I could not marry a man who doesn't share my beliefs. I think this relationship has gone as far as it can go."

"But Angelica, I love you. I have never felt this way about any other woman. You are perfect for me."

"I'm sorry. I want a man that is not only devoted to me, but also to my church. I want children we could proudly raise to be good examples of church members."

TJ whispered, "I can't be that man." He got up from the lunch table, emptied his tray into the proper receptacle, and retreated to his next class. He couldn't believe that his first and only romance was over.

After all of his classes were over, he went to the GYM and swam laps until he was so tired that he could hardly swim another stroke.

Coach Andrews could tell something was wrong, so he encouraged TJ to keep swimming. He knew that was a good way to quell his anxiety and come back to be the boy he knew and loved.

"TJ, continue swimming until your problems disappear."

The swimmer got out of the water, toweled off, got dressed and headed back to the dorm. He wanted to think. He didn't want to talk to anyone.

* * * * *

TJ spent all of his time either swimming or studying for his classes. He felt really depressed. He knew he would have a difficult time getting over Angelica. He had never been in love before and now his heart had been broken.

Why did she break up with him because he wasn't a member of her church? Why was her church so important to her?

He knew he had to concentrate on himself and try to forget about her.

He signed up for Culinary I. He was looking forward to that.

Hopefully, Angelica will have it at a different time. Cooking was always a number one priority, he knew he needed to think about becoming a great chef when he could no longer compete in swimming. When he was thinking about swimming, the Olympics and his culinary abilities, his depression seemed to lessen.

* * * * *

Coach Andrews cornered TJ after one of his routine swimming sessions.

"TJ, I'd like to talk to you. I can tell you have some kind of problem."

"No I'm fine. I'm looking forward to Olympic tryouts next year."

"There's something else that's wrong. I can tell. Do you want to talk about it?" Coach Andrews asked.

"No, I'm fine. I just need to concentrate on my swimming and academics. Those things keep me busy and I need to focus on them."

"Okay, but remember I am here if you need someone to talk to."

"Thanks, I will remember that," TJ acknowledged.

He went back to his room, made a light meal and laid down and went to sleep. His aching heart went away when he was asleep.

* * * * *

Joe got in touch with TJ the next week. His romance was on the fritz also. "My partner decided he did not want to be with me anymore. He was looking for a new interest."

"I met the love of my life and she dumped me. She didn't like it because I didn't want to join her church. I'm definitely not looking for another relationship at this time. Maybe never," TJ explained.

"We had some good times together. Maybe we could make it work this time," Joe said thoughtfully.

"Sorry, Joe I'm not interested. I don't mean to sound rude, but please find someone else."

Joe gave TJ a big hug, then turned around and retreated out the door.

TJ tried concentrating on his book, but to no avail. He decided to go for a walk. He headed down the main street until he came to the Malt Shop. He looked in the window and then decided to go in. Maybe a chocolate malt would make him feel better.

He walked up to the counter. There standing behind the counter was Angelica. She commented, "Hi, TJ you look awful. Forgive me, I didn't mean it the way it sounded. You look like you could use a good night's sleep. What can I get for you?"

"Nothing, I guess I made a mistake coming here. I didn't know you were working here."

TJ turned around and walked back out the door.

Angelica called after him, "TJ, I'm sorry if I hurt you. I didn't mean to. You are a great guy, I wish things could have turned out differently."

"That's ok. I am just having a hard time understanding the whole thing."

He continued his walk out the door, not looking back.

He decided to go back to the dorm.

* * * * *

After seeing Angelica, he was starting to feel better about himself and everything that had happened. Somehow he realized the break-up with Angelica was not his fault. He had done nothing wrong. He knew he had to get over his feelings of inadequacy.

The next day he thought he was prepared for anything. For some unknown reason, when he got to his English class, the professor spoke on the topic of "Feelings of Inadequacy". He didn't know if he could sit through listening to someone approach the subject he had just been thinking about.

The professor started by telling that everybody had feelings of inadequacy at some time in his or her life. And that the person needs to get to the root of what was making that person feel inadequate.

Many thoughts started running through his mind, to the point that he was not paying attention to the class leader. However, he did come to the conclusion that he was as good as anyone else he knew. "I am intelligent, thoughtful, loving and most of all I am a good person."

When TJ got back to his room, he noticed there was a letter from his Mom waiting for him. He opened it up hurriedly. He always looked forward to letters from home.

Dear TJ,

We just wanted to let you know how much we enjoyed the visit from you and Angelica. We are looking forward to seeing the two of you soon. You really know how to pick them. She is perfect for you. I hope that soon you will bring her home to show her with a ring on her finger. She will make you a great wife. Dad and I hope to see both of you soon.

Love,
Mom and Dad

TJ felt like crying, but he didn't. How was he going to tell his parents that there wouldn't be a marriage between him and her? What was a nice way to say he had been dumped?

He wasn't going to think about that yet. He would have to sleep on it.

When he awoke, he still didn't feel like writing to them. Maybe at lunch, or after supper tonight. I have to tell them, but how?

* * * * *

He got his swimming time in, both morning before classes and also after supper. He just didn't have the words to tell them. It wasn't going to be easy. He kept rehearsing over and over the words he would use. Nothing seemed right. I have to tell them. Maybe tomorrow.

Joe came to see him again. He asked, "Would you like to go to the Malt Shop and get a chocolate malt? Chocolate always helps me when I'm depressed. Hopefully it will help you, too. I hate to see you down like this.

TJ asked, "How are you doing with your swimming sessions? I haven't seen you at the pool lately."

"I quit that class. I wasn't doing very well, so I didn't see any sense in continuing. Do you still want to try out for the Olympics next year?" He asked, changing the subject.

"I see your grammar hasn't improved either," TJ noted.

"Huh?"

"Never mind. Yes I am still aiming for the Olympic try outs," TJ answered. "Coach Andrews thinks I have a good chance."

"Would you like to go for a walk and talk for a while?" Joe suggested.

"Not really. I have homework and a thesis to hand in on Monday. I need to concentrate on that," TJ admitted.

"Okay, I can take a hint. I'll see you later," Joe said with a big hug.

"See you, Joe."

TJ decided this would be a good time to write back to Mom and Dad. 'I know how disappointed they will be. They ought to be on this end.'

He reached for pen and paper:

Dear Mom and Dad,

Things didn't work out the way we wanted. Angelica said she would only marry a Mormon. I told her I wasn't ready to join any church.

She broke up with me. I saw her at the Malt Shop. It turns out, she is working there. I thought maybe a chocolate malt would be good about that time. We exchanged pleasantries and I went back to my room without a malt.

I'm sorry I didn't write sooner, I've been really depressed. I thought she was the one I would spend the rest of my life with. Not so.

So now, I am concentrating on my swimming and my scholastics. I need to get great grades so I can try out for the Olympics next year. I must do my very best in everything.

I don't think I will be home for a while. I have too many memories of my visit there with Angelica.

I send you my love and hope you understand how I feel.

Love,
TJ

He read the letter again and decided it was the best he could do under the circumstances. The envelope was addressed and stamped. He would drop it in the mail box in the morning.

TEN

Time seemed to go fast. Maybe too fast. Olympic try outs were here. Was he ready? He'll soon find out.

Coach Andrews insured him that he was ready. He knew everything he was supposed to know. However, TJ must still go through the initial trials. He couldn't help being nervous. The Coach just watched and encourage him.

TJ was at his best weight and strength. The coach would push him more and more until he didn't think he could work out any harder, but he did. He knew he had a chance to be in the Olympics, but there were always doubts in the back of his head. Was he good enough?

He knew he must have a dependable job. He had to support himself while also finding enough time to train. He got a job as a librarian at the largest library in the state.

Getting hours in the library and the pool would be hard but he knew he could do it. He knew he must do it. This was his whole life. This is all he had seriously thought about since he was small.

Dad did not understand. He was hoping his son would be in football, baseball, basketball or even soccer. That was not what TJ wanted. He had always been interested in swimming. Swimming was graceful, beautiful, and most of all a great sport. Yes, sport. Dad didn't consider swimming a sport. That it was a recreation.

Coach Andrews was a great coach. He spotted TJ's love of the sport when he was new in college. He would spend hours teaching him techniques, and watching him master each one. However, if he were seriously considering being on the Olympic team, he must swim more. He must swim 100 hours a week. That is a hard regimen to try to follow. That is the hard regimen he must follow if he wants to achieve his goal.

* * * * *

He was not able to spend time at home. He would try to write them a letter once a week.

He swam in as many competitions as possible. He did quite well, however, he hadn't won any. He got very little recognition. Once in a while a scout would talk to Coach Andrews, but TJ knew he had to work harder to gain the right recognition.

Finally, a scout told Coach Andrews that he thought TJ had a lot of potential. He still had to swim harder and smarter. He must reach his goal of 100 hours of swimming a week. It was hard on him and just as hard on Coach Andrews. He also had to spend hours at the pool watching TJ carefully. He had to look for mistakes and help TJ correct them.

Joe was also swimming alongside of TJ. He knew he would never be as good as his friend, but he encouraged him any way he could. He never seemed to leave his side.

TJ wasn't able to continue with his culinary class. He would have to start again when he was finished with the Olympics and getting endorsements to help pay for his dreams of earning many gold medals.

The two friends got an apartment together with Joe paying his share.

* * * * *

TJ started winning a few meets. He could feel he was doing better. That same scout was keeping an eye on TJ. He could see his potential.

The scout approached Coach Andrews, "That's quite a boy you have there. My name is Travis O'Malley. I'm interested in him. I know a couple of clients that might endorse him. Do you think he might be interested?"

"I think he just might. He's interested in getting on the Olympic Swim Team. I'm sure I could talk to him about some endorsements. Give me your card and I will have a chat with TJ and find out if he is interested."

The two men shook hands and Travis O'Malley left the Gym.

When TJ got out of the pool and started toweling off, Coach Andrews approached him. He had a big grin on his face. The swimmer looked skeptical. "What's going on? Who was the man you were talking with?"

All the coach could do was grin.

"Tell me, Coach, what's going on? It must be good. In all the time of your coaching, I have never seen you grin like that," TJ admitted.

"A scout has had his eye on you, and he thinks you have potential. He's talking about getting you some endorsements. Do you have any idea how wonderful that would be? Without endorsements, there could be no Olympics for you. If you get the endorsements you need, the Olympics is only a year away. That means you are going to have to work harder than you ever have in your life. You think I have been hard on you? You haven't seen anything yet."

Joe was standing near enough to hear what had been said. He grabbed TJ and gave him a big hug and then kissed him square on the lips.

At first TJ didn't know what to think, then he embraced his friend and held tight.

The thrill of the moment had gotten the best of both men. Then TJ embraced Coach Andrews. It seemed to be a natural thing to do. Coach Andrews hugged him back. They were all so happy.

"You go home and get a good night's sleep. I expect to see you back here at 4:30. Don't eat before you get here. You can eat after the workout I am going to put you through," as he directed his instructions to TJ.

"Yes, Coach, I'll be here and raring to get started."

* * * * *

The walk back to his apartment with Joe was very quiet. All he could think about was the swimming regimen, endorsements, and the Olympics next year. Could he do this? Of course he could and he WILL.

Joe tried to hold hands with TJ as they walked, but he had other more important things on his mind.

Joe was excited because he had been able to kiss his friend. But did TJ understand that the kiss was not just because of the excitement of the moment, but it was out of love. He knew that his friend would know soon.

* * * * *

TJ said to Joe, "I'm so excited. I have to write to Mom and Dad and let them know of my encounter with Coach Andrews this evening."

"Don't forget what the coach said about getting a good night's sleep," Joe reminded TJ.

"I could never forget anything Coach Andrews said tonight."

As they entered the apartment Joe said, "I am going to bed now," after a huge made-up yawn.

"I will write a quick note to Mom and then I will go to bed too."

With the letter to his mom completed, he got into his pajamas and crawled into bed, hoping to fall asleep quickly. As luck would have it, his mind was racing and he still couldn't think of anything but that night's happening. He turned with his face toward the wall. Joe couldn't wait any longer. He carefully climbed in bed with TJ. He put his arm around his soon-to-be lover's waist and held him. TJ knew what was happening, but he enjoyed cuddling. They slept that way all night. TJ didn't know what he was feeling. Could it have been this way with Angelica? Probably not.

The alarm went off at 4:00. TJ pushed Joe aside so he could get up and turn the alarm off. Joe could sleep longer if he wanted to, but TJ knew he had to get dressed and get his swimming gear together and head out the door. It was chilly outside, but the walk was invigorating. He had barely gotten down the outside steps of his apartment when Joe was beside him. "You could have slept longer. You didn't need to come with me so early."

Joe said, "I wanted to come with you. I hope you don't mind."

"No, that's fine, it's just so early."

They reached the Gym and opened the door to find Coach Andrews. "Great, I'm glad to see you follow my instructions so eagerly."

"Of course, I want this more than anything in the world. I feel like nothing can stop me as long as I have you in my corner. Let's get started."

The coach said, "Good. Give me 5 laps to get warmed up."

TJ was already in his trunks and cap. He dived into the Olympic sized pool and started his regimen.

He was in the pool until 7:00. Joe stayed in until about 6:00 and then waited on the edge of the pool.

Then Coach Andrews said, "Go home and have a hearty breakfast. How long do you have to work at the library?"

"Till 5:00."

"Okay, I expect you back here at 5:45. And in your trunks and cap by 6:00."

"Yes, Sir!" with emphasis on the Sir.

* * * * *

TJ swam every day, even Sunday. He wanted to go to see his parents for a weekend, but that wasn't feasible. He had to put every moment available into working on his strokes. There were so many different strokes, he didn't know how many he could master. But with the help of his great coach, he figured anything was possible.

Luckily, he didn't have time to think about Angelica. She was no longer in his life, but he still had that ache. He felt she was the only woman he would ever love. But now he could only concentrate on getting into the Olympics next year. Right now that seemed like an impossibility.

Every evening Travis O'Malley would show up to check on TJ's progress. He would stand and talk to Coach Andrews. He never showed any emotion. He would stroke his chin, as if he were looking for a mosquito that was on his face. Then he would leave, never to be seen until the next evening.

When TJ was finished with the night's routine, he would talk to the coach while he was drying off. "Did Mr. O'Malley have anything interesting to say about me? Or maybe some prospects for endorsements?"

"Not really. He did say he could see improvement in your technique. That was about all. He has been speaking with a couple of company heads that might be interested in endorsing some enterprising young man like you."

"Are you serious? That's wonderful. I know, don't get my hopes up."

"That's right, and besides, I doubt if you are the only athlete he is looking at. Because he is here just about every evening, he must be very interested in you."

TJ beamed. Joe was always on the sideline to help boost his morale.

Joe and TJ walked back to their apartment. Joe reached for TJ's hand, but his friend just pulled away. He wasn't sure of his feelings for Joe. As far as he knew, they were just good friends.

The nightly routine was the same when they returned to their beds. TJ liked to cuddle. He liked the closeness to somebody, but he wasn't ready for anything else. This went on for months.

TJ was feeling trapped. He needed some space. He decided to ask the coach if he could take a weekend off. Coach Andrew could tell that the man was feeling stressed. "I think it would be a good idea if you went to have a relaxing weekend with your parents."

"Thanks, Coach, I'll be back at 5:00 Monday morning." TJ shook his hand hard and after he was dressed, he and Joe left.

Joe said, "It will be nice to see your parents again. It's been a long time."

"Sorry, Joe. I'm going alone. I want to be relaxed for a couple of days. I need to get a few things straight in my mind. I'm confused. Please understand."

"I don't, but I will give you your space," Joe said disheartened.

ELEVEN

Saturday was a gloomy day. He hadn't informed his parents that he was coming. He was still feeling stressed about his feelings and Travis O'Malley and Coach Andrews.

As he pulled up the driveway, his mother had been looking out the kitchen window. She rushed out to greet him. "You should have told me you were coming. I must look a mess."

"Mom, you don't have to dress up for me. I'm your son."

"I know. Your dad is out in the field somewhere. He will be so excited to see you."

"Mom, I need a good rest without many questions. I feel like I want to be alone, like the good old days when life was easier."

"Take all the time you need. We can talk anytime you are ready."

"You are the best Mom in the world. I knew I could come here and you would accept me under any conditions and love me for who I am."

"Go up to your room and rest. We will talk later."

TJ did just that. He could not sleep, but just lying on his bed was a big comfort. He had to think about what he was going to say to his parents. Would they understand? Would they judge? He was so confused, he didn't know what to say or how to say it.

* * * * *

Tom came home for lunch and saw TJ's car in the driveway. "Where is our boy?"

"He isn't a boy, Tom. He is a troubled man. He needed to get away from all of the things that are making him stress," Janet said.

"I don't know why he would be stressed. He has so much going for him. His swimming career, a great coach, a job, his own apartment, and Joe to help him pay for the expenses. Why would he be stressed?"

"We will have to wait and see what he says."

"Maybe I should stay home this afternoon and talk to him," Tom thought out loud.

"No, you go back to what you were doing. He may not come down until supper anyway."

Tom sullenly ate his lunch and went back to his chores.

Soon after his dad left, TJ came down stairs to find his mother in the kitchen, as usual.

"Mom, can we talk," TJ asked. His hair was messy, not the way he usually came down. Something was certainly not right.

"Of course," his mother answered.

"Mom, I think I might be gay."

Janet sat down with a thud. "What makes you think that?"

"Joe has been living with me and he ends up in my bed every night."

"Have you had sex?" She almost chocked on the words.

"No, not yet. So far it has been just cuddling. I find I like to cuddle. I'm sure Joe would like more. I'm just not ready for that. I am so confused. I like Joe, but I don't love him. I haven't loved anyone since Angelica."

"Do you think Joe loves you?"

"Yes, he has said he does. I am hoping I will be able to love someone again. I just don't know if I am gay or straight. No other girls have appealed to me. Men don't appeal to me either. I'm looking for love, but I am so confused. I don't know what I want. I need this weekend to help make decisions. I don't want to lose Joe as a friend or as a roommate. For one thing, I don't know if I would be able to afford my apartment without Joe's help. I don't know what to do."

"Have you thought about trying to get back with Angelica? You love her."

"Yes, I love her, but I am not ready to become a Mormon just to make her happy. I'm not sure that would make me happy."

"Would becoming a Mormon be so terrible?"

"I don't know. They have a lot of strict rules. I don't know if I could live up to that. Besides, maybe she has already found someone else."

"You won't know if you don't ask."

"I don't have time to romance anyone right now. I am going to try out for the Olympics. My coach says I'm ready. That has been my goal ever since I can remember. The scout, Travis O'Malley, is looking for endorsements for me. I cannot even think about the Olympics without endorsements. Mr. O'Malley has been to all of my practices and meets. I'm on overload. I haven't even had time to think. What do I want?"

"That's the decision you are going to have to make. Is it the Olympics or Culinary School? Is it Joe or Angelica? You have a hard road to travel."

"Yes I have. If I decide to quit my goal for the Olympics, I will hurt Coach Andrews and probably myself. If I decide to pursue Angelica will I be happy? If I stay with Joe and forget about Angelica will I be happy? My confusion is driving me nuts. What should I do, Mom?"

"I can't make those decisions. Only you can. And make them carefully. Don't let others persuade you in either direction."

"Thank you. You are the best mother in the world."

"Just remember that I love you unconditionally. No matter what you decide, I will always love you. I might not like your choice, but I will always be there for you. You can always talk to me."

"I know. Now I have to talk to Dad," TJ moaned.

"Yes, now I want to make a special supper. It won't hurt to soften your Dad up before any serious matters can be brought up. After a delicious dessert, then you and he can talk."

"You'll be there for the conversation, won't you?"

Janet paused and then said, "Wouldn't you rather talk to your Dad alone?"

"No, maybe you could run interference for me."

"I really think you should speak to your dad alone. You know, Man to Man."

"That scares me to death. I want you near so you can voice your opinion."

"All right I will stay here, but if the conversation gets heated, I may bow out."

"I respect that," TJ said, "even though it may get rough."

* * * * *

Tom came in from having worked especially hard. As soon as he saw TJ, he practically ran to him and hugged him with all his might.

Then sniffing the air said, "That smells like ham. What's the occasion?"

Janet explained, "I just thought it would be nice to fix a good meal now that the Prodigal Son has returned."

"Prodigal Son, huh?" Tom was being sarcastic. "What's up, son? Have you and Angelica decided to get married, after all?"

TJ said, "Let's eat. I'm starving."

After the hearty meal, TJ looking down stated, "We need to talk."

The trio at the table looked somber.

"Okay, Son, I'm listening."

"Dad," TJ stammered, "I think I might be gay."

Tom replied, "That's impossible. No one in my family has ever been gay." He had a hard time reacting to a statement like that.

"Dad, it's not a disease. It's something that sometimes happens."

"Something horrible like that has to be a disease. No, no one in this family has ever had this happen. You are my son, not some monstrosity like that. No you are not gay. I will not accept that. I don't even want to hear about it. It will not be allowed in this house. How could I tell the rest of the family that my son is gay? No, this cannot be. What about Angelica? Does she know this?"

"Dad, we broke up some time ago. Of course, she doesn't know. I came out here to let you know my feelings."

"Your feelings?" he said as he pounded his fist on the table.

"I won't have it. No, I just won't accept the idea that MY SON is gay. That is not the way we raised you. I tried to be sure that you would always be a man, not some freak."

"I'm sorry you feel that way. This is not the life I chose for myself. I'm not even sure I am gay. I'm confused."

Janet sat very quiet. She was beginning to want to stay out of the conversation, but Tom dragged her in. "Janet, how do you feel about this?"

Very quietly she said, "TJ and I have already discussed it. He had to have time to talk to you."

Tom motioned to TJ, "So talk. Let me know your feelings."

"I don't want to get into an argument. I want to keep it cordial," the son stated.

"How can we not have an argument? This thing is so wrong."

TJ came back with, "This may seem so wrong to you, but wouldn't you want to know how I feel?"

"I think it's more important how your mother and I feel about all this," dad proclaimed.

"I think you have made that very clear how you feel. What do you know about how Mom feels?"

"Of course, she feels the same way I do," Dad said.

"Mom, how do you feel? Tell Dad."

"I don't want to start World War Three. I have told you how I feel. I'm not in favor of you being gay, but I will always love you no matter which way you chose to go."

"I don't believe I'm hearing this. How can you love a son who thinks he might be gay?" Dad asked.

"I gave birth to him twenty years ago. I will always love him. It cannot be any other way. I love you," she admitted to Dad, "but I don't always agree with the choices you make."

"What does that mean?" Tom enquired.

"I don't want to get into that. The subject we have to consider is TJ."

"TJ, do you have a boyfriend?" was Dad's question.

"Yes, and before you asked, we have never had sex, although the opportunity has risen many times. I'm not ready for that," TJ expressed.

Then trying to change the subject a bit, Tom asked "What about Angelica?"

"As I told Mom, Angelica broke up with me because I wouldn't change to Mormonism. She won't marry a man that is not a Mormon. That's her choice. I am not ready to change to any religion."

"So, is that the reason you think you might want to be gay?" Dad asked out of the blue.

"Right now, I don't know what I want. That is the reason I came here to talk to you and Mom. I'm confused."

Tom related, "So am I. This has been an exhausting evening. I think we should all go to bed. Maybe that will give us time to come to some decisions."

* * * * *

TJ went to his room. He didn't like the direction the evening had taken. He was still confused. He didn't know how he was supposed to feel or what he should do. He loves both of his parents, he loves swimming, and he likes Joe. That is the big dilemma. He likes Joe, but he still loves Angelica. What to do? What to do?

* * * * *

When he awoke, he decided the route he should take. He must speak to his dad before he leaves the house for the morning chores.

He dressed and descended the stairs. He could hear his parents talking softly in the kitchen.

When they saw him, all became quiet. Of course, they had been talking about him, otherwise, the talking would not have stopped.

"I didn't sleep well at all last night. I had a lot on my mind. I'm glad you are still here. I would like you to hear what I have to say before I go back to the city.

"Well, to start with, I'm pretty sure I am not gay. If Joe wants to continue to help with the rent on our apartment, there will be some rules. He will have to sleep in his own bed, in his own room. If that isn't acceptable, he will have to find an apartment of his own.

"Next, I will go to Coach Andrews and thank him for all he has done for me. I'm sure he will not be happy. No more Olympic goal. No more Mr. O'Malley looking for endorsements for me.

"Then, I will resume my ambition to become a great chef. Culinary I here I come."

Tom tried to interrupt, but TJ lifted his hand to let everyone know he wasn't finished.

"I have always loved being in the kitchen, and I think I have a good chance of becoming a great chef.

"After that decision, I've been thinking about seeing if Angelica will take me back. I feel like she is the only one I will ever love, at least at this point. If she will not give me another chance, I will have to keep my eye open for another woman. One that will love me for who I am. And not have a lot of expectations from me."

Tom decided this was the time to let TJ know about his feelings.

"Son, I am proud of you. I feel you are aware of who you were, and are ready to assume a new way of thinking."

TJ smiled, "Thanks Dad. I'm ready to become the new Thomas Allen Williams, Junior. I'm sorry I can't become the athlete you would have liked me to be. I have never leaned toward being an athlete. I realize that I think I could be very content working side-by-side with others in the food industry."

Tom surprised TJ by saying, "I think you have made the right decision. Your maturity astounds me. As I said before, I am proud of the man you have become. I think your mother feels the same way."

Janet had tears in her eyes. "I knew if I didn't pressure you, that the right consequences would come out. Yes, I am proud of you too."

TJ hugged them both and then announced, "I am going to leave now. I have a lot of damage to rectify. None of it will be easy. I think the sooner I get back to my apartment, the sooner I can start my new life."

"I agree," Janet stated emphatically. The tears were still flowing.

"I'll let you know how everything turns out." Then he went around the corner into the living room and picked up his suitcase. He set it down in the kitchen and gave his parents one more tight hug and kissed his mother on her tear stained face and shook hands with his dad. He bid them good-bye and picked his suitcase up once more and went out the kitchen door to his car.

When he left the driveway he too, started to cry. He had made some errors, but he was ready to start over. A new TJ.

TWELVE

TJ cried all the way back to the city.

When he pulled into his parking space, he sat for a few minutes, trying to compose himself. He must speak with Joe first. Joe had a surprise coming to him. He walked carefully up the stairs for the fourth floor. 401 He hesitated before he opened the door. He liked his apartment. He didn't have much furniture, only the necessities, a couch, a stuffed chair. In the dinette a small table and two chairs, a stove and a small refrigerator. In his bedroom he had a bed and a dresser. That's all.

TJ knew Joe would be in the living room waiting for him. This was not going to be easy.

"Hi, Joe", TJ said when he opened the door.

"Hi, I'm glad you made it home safely. You're back a little sooner than I expected. How are your parents?"

"My parents are great. I came home a little early because I want to have a serious talk with you, and to Coach Andrews."

"Hmm, that sounds kinda suspicious," Joe said.

"I was hoping you would be home. I wanted to talk to you first," TJ related.

"Things are going to change around here. We have two bedrooms. One for you and one for me. There is not going to be any 'Hanky Panky'. There will never be any love between us. If you are looking for a sexual relationship, you'll have to find it someplace else. And you cannot bring a lover here. I am straight and I am going to stay that way. Those are my rules. If you do not want to live those rules, then you will have to find another apartment. As long as you are willing to live under MY rules, then you can stay here. If you are not happy, move out."

"Wow, that was unexpected. I thought we were closer than that," Joe stated.

"No, we're not. I would like you to continue to be my friend, but that's all. I really like you. And I mean LIKE. There is no love associated with that. Give a good deal of thought about that, and give me an answer next week. I'm not kicking you out, I'm giving you a choice. It's up to you."

"I'm going to see Angelica and find out if we can get back together. I love her," TJ said.

"Okay, I see where you're coming from. I've upset you. I will stay here until you change your mind. I can be patient," Joe said almost tearfully.

"I'm going to bed. I have a lot to think about. Good-night, Joe."

Joe had a lot to think about, too. 'What had happened while TJ was at his parent's farm? I know, they talked him into thinking he is straight. That has to be it. He wouldn't have come to this conclusion on his own. I'll give him some space. Sooner or later he will come to his senses and realize we belong together.'

* * * * *

TJ had a fretful night sleep. He tossed and turned thinking how he was going to explain to Coach Andrews about his decision. The coach had done so much for him. He had stood behind him in every situation; taught him strokes, stood behind him at all his meets, encouraged him when he was down and been with him in good times. Coach Andrews was like a second father to TJ. Now he felt like he was letting him down. Actually, he was letting him down. In a way, he was also letting himself down. He had wanted to be a great swimmer and an Olympian. He had worked so hard to achieve his goals. Yes, this was a real dilemma.

The night passed so slowly, TJ couldn't make up his mind as to how he was going to approach Coach Andrews.

Four o'clock finally arrived. The time to face Coach Andrews was eminent.

He got out of bed and dressed, but not in his swim gear. He walked slowly to the Gym. The lights were on. He knew Coach Andrews was waiting for his protégé to come through the doors.

As TJ walked into the pool area, he could see his mentor waiting for him near the edge of the pool.

The coach looked surprised when he saw that TJ was not ready to do laps.

"TJ, why aren't you ready to swim this morning? I thought you would be anxious to get started. It has been three days since you were last in the pool."

"Coach, I want to talk to you. There have been changes and I want to try and explain them to you." TJ gulped hard and tried to get his composure. "I'm not going to swim on the team anymore. I am quitting all together. It has been a difficult decision, but one I have to live with."

The coach stated, "You can't do this. You have come so far. You have made me so proud. You have been, by far, my best student. I have worked so hard to get you to this point, where you can compete with confidence and win some meets.

"What about the Olympics? I thought that was your goal. You want to give all of that up?"

"I went to see my parents this weekend because I was confused about a number of things. Swimming and the Olympics was one of the things that I was troubled about. It started when I was thinking about what I was going to do once I could no longer compete. I would still be young enough to have another career. But, what? This may sound silly to you, because it is so far from my swimming. Sure I could go on TV and endorse items in commercials. No, not for me. I want to make something for myself now.

"Being home with my parents made me realize that I spent hours in the kitchen with my mother, doing everything from cooking, to baking, roasting, and cleaning up after myself. I decided that I should go to Culinary School and become the best chef I can become."

Coach Andrews laughed, "Become a chef? I don't think you are realizing the mistake you would be making. You need to take some more time, away from your parents, and give this much more thought. You would be giving up your lifelong dream of becoming an Olympian Gold Medal Champion. You could do it, you know. You have that dream in sight. You can't just give up this opportunity. You have greatness in you. I've seen it ever since you came to this college. You know, you will lose your scholarship?"

"Yes, I realize how much I will be giving up, but I need to be happy. I want to make ME happy. This is the decision I have made, and I am not going to change my mind. It has not been an easy decision. I have thought about it for some time. I have not really been myself. I want to be loved for who I am, not for what people want me to be."

"I'm sorry that you are willing to give up everything for the silly thing you think you want to do. Like I said take some more time and make sure this is the right decision. I will gladly take you back into the program. You are the best student I have ever had."

"Thank you, Coach, I appreciate that. I know I couldn't have had a better coach," TJ complimented the gracious man. "I have one more stop to make. You are the best."

* * * * *

It will be a few hours before he could go to the Malt Shop to see Angelica. She may not be there until her classes end. He decided he might just as well go back to his apartment. He figured Joe would be there. He wasn't anxious to encounter him again this morning.

He unlocked the door. The apartment was empty. Joe must have gone to his classes. 'Good! Hopefully I will have some time to myself.'

He got a couple of books out. He knew he was behind in his academics. He had missed several days. He was sure he could make them up quickly.

He opened his calculus theory book. He found where he should be and got a pencil and paper to take notes. He soon was slumped over his arms on top of the book. He had fallen asleep. It was no wonder. He hadn't slept well last night, worrying about all of his problems.

When he awoke, it was lunch time. He decided to see the Head Dean, Professor Danbury.

He combed his hair. It was messy because of falling asleep as he had. He must look his best when going to see the Dean of the College.

He walked back to the school and to the Dean's office. He walked in and was greeted by a secretary. "Can I help you, Young Man?"

"Yes, I would like to see Dean Danbury. My name is Thomas Williams."

"One moment, please. She pushed the button on the intercom. "Sir, there is a gentleman here to see you."

A voice returned, "What is his name?"

The secretary announced, "Thomas Williams."

"Does he have an appointment?" came the question.

"No, Sir. He asked to see you."

"Please show him in."

The secretary opened the door and TJ entered. He shook hands with the man sitting behind the desk. "Sir, I am dropping a class and I would like to start another."

"Let me look at your records. Miss B (short for Birmingham), Please bring me Thomas' records."

"Yes, Sir, right away." Miss B soon returned with a couple of manila folders. Then she handed them to the Dean.

He looked them over carefully. "I see by your transcripts that you are an excellent student."

"Thank you, Sir," was the reply.

"What class do you want to drop?" the Dean asked.

"Swimming, Sir,"

"Are you sure? Have you given enough time to be sure? This is a huge change. I've spoken to Coach Andrews, and he told me about your aspirations. He thinks the Olympics are in your future. Are you willing to give that up?" Dean Danbury explained.

"I am very sure. I spoke to Coach Andrews just this morning." TJ tried to reassure the Dean. "I am extremely serious about this change. I am trying to start my life over. I don't want to be known as the kid that could have been. I want to be known as the kid who went all the way to becoming the best in his field."

"Just what is the field that you want to be the best at?" the Dean enquired.

"Culinary, Sir," TJ said proudly. "I think I can be the best in anything I endeavor to do."

"I think you are right. Let me overlook the rosters. Hmm. It looks like there aren't any openings in Culinary I. Either we will have to wait for someone to opt out, or we will have to wait for the new semester."

"I can wait," TJ was optimistic. "I know this is the career I want to pursue."

"I will stand behind you in your goal. I will even see if there is a grant available in your field, since you will be losing your swimming grants," Dean Danbury said as he extended his hand to shake TJ's.

"Thank you, Sir, you have been a great help for me. With you behind me, how can anything go wrong?" TJ grinned the biggest grin he had ever exerted.

"Now, I have one more stop to make before I return to my apartment for a huge night of studying."

* * * * *

He was feeling elated after speaking with Dean Danbury. He hoped his next encounter would go as well.

He walked to the Malt Shop. It had just opened for business. As he walked in, he didn't see Angelica. Maybe it wasn't time for her shift. He sat down at the bar and ordered a Latte. When it was presented to him, he asked the gentleman, "Does Angelica still work here?"

"Yes, but she will not be in until 4:00. She works until we close at 10:00," was the answer.

"Thanks," as he addressed the waiter.

"Are you a friend of hers?" asked the gentleman.

"I'd like to think so. At least I want to be," TJ said.

TJ slowly finished his Latte and headed for the door. He still had several hours before he could talk to Angelica. So he went to his apartment and took a short nap. He felt invigorated, so he reached for one of his books and started reading where he had left off.

He looked at the clock. Three fifty. He had better start for the Malt Shop. Maybe she would be there a little early so they could talk.

He walked briskly, he really wanted to speak to her right away.

As he reached for the door, Angelica reached at the same time.

"Hi, Angelica. I would like to talk to you," TJ had rehearsed what he wanted to say to her many times, but now he felt tongue-tied.

She was more beautiful than he had remembered.

"It doesn't look very busy yet. I think we can chat for a few moments," Angelica beamed as she looked at TJ. She put her apron on and went to her station behind the bar. "What would you like to talk to me about?"

"You and me," he was shaking like a leaf.

"Have there been any changes lately?" Angelica was very nervous also.

"As a matter of fact, yes. I went to my parent's house last weekend. I had a very serious talk with them. I was confused and I figured if I went home, I might be able to make things seem right again. One thing I decided was to quit the Swim Team. That didn't seem important anymore. I always wanted to be on the Olympic Swim Team, but no longer. If I want to see the Olympics I can watch it on TV. I spoke to Coach Andrews early this morning and told him of my decision. He was sad, but respected me for choosing to go a different direction.

"Then I went to see Dean Danbury to let him know of my decision to drop the Swim Team and choose to take Culinary I. He said he would help me anyway he can. There isn't an opening in the Culinary School right now, but as soon as there is an opening, he would help me get in. I may have to wait until a new semester.

That's ok, I'm patient."

"Next, I wanted to see you. I don't know how you feel about me, but you are the only girl I have ever loved. I would like to see us get back together."

Angelica was stunned. She didn't know what to say. She thought a moment and then attacked the situation, "TJ, I think we could have had a wonderful time together, but you know my feelings about marrying a Mormon. That hasn't changed."

"I didn't think it had. I've thought that over, and I would like to take the lessons. If I decide to become a member of your church, would I have a chance with you?"

Angelica thought for about two minutes, then replied, "I could not marry you if I thought the only reason you joined my church was to marry me. I really thought we had a good time together and that there was a chance you would love my church, too. But now I'm not so sure."

"I thought your church was interesting, but at that time I was not ready to join any church. After speaking to my parents, and seeing how much they love you, I realized that I will love you forever, even if you decide you do not want to marry me."

"Actually, I have been seeing someone else. He is a member of my church. He just got back from his mission to Canada. There has been nothing serious between us. We've just been going out casually. I'm not in love with him, yet. We just have a good time together."

"Do you think you would like to give us a try again? I would take the lessons from the missionaries, and if I felt it was the right church, I would join. If not, we could go our separate ways," TJ said seriously.

Angelica said very calmly, "We'll see, I have to have time to really consider everything you have said. Now, I have to get to work. I don't want to lose my job," she said as she smiled. "See you later."

"You can take all the time you need. When you have made some kind of conclusion, we can meet at the cafeteria. You can give me your answer, yea or nay. I'll wait for your answer, whether next week, next month or next year. I will wait."

She went to help a customer and TJ walked out the door and walked back to his apartment.

THIRTEEN

TJ crammed his books for hours on end. That was the only thing to keep his mind off of Angelica. He figured he would concentrate on the courses he had left after dumping the Swim Team. He couldn't get into Culinary I for a while, so he worked hard on the classes he still had. He was a good student. He knew he wouldn't be behind very long. He went to each Professor and copied the lessons he was behind. His Professors were very gracious. Because he had been doing so well in his subjects, each one was willing to give him a chance to catch up. He knew it was only a matter of time before he was completely up with the rest of his classmates.

Angelica was still foremost on his mind. He wanted her back so badly.

He wondered if she were taking Culinary I. Wouldn't that be wonderful if they could take that class together.

* * * * *

Joe kept his distance. When he came to the apartment, they would exchange pleasantries, "Hi TJ, how are you doing?" "Hi Joe, I'm fine. How are you?" The answers were always the same. There was nothing personal in their greetings.

* * * * *

Weeks went by and he didn't hear from Dean Danbury. He didn't hear from Angelica either. Maybe that was her way of telling him that there was someone else in her life, and there wasn't any room for him. He tried to date other girls, but he knew that was futile, there couldn't be anyone else.

It was ironic, Angelica wouldn't marry anyone who wasn't a Mormon and TJ wouldn't marry anyone who wasn't a good cook.

* * * * *

TJ got a call from the Dean's Office that there was an opening in Culinary I. So as soon as his class was over in which he was in, he rushed to the Dean's Office.

The secretary smiled when he walked in, "Hello, Mr. Williams. I'll let the Dean know you are here."

"Thank you Miss B."

Miss B. contacted the Dean over the intercom. TJ could hear him say, "Send him right in."

TJ didn't wait for Miss B. to tell him to go in. He was at the door before the Dean was finished answering Miss B's request.

He knocked softly on the door and then entered.

Dean Danbury had a big smile on his face, "Please be seated Tom. I have some good news for you. There has been an opening in Culinary I. It is from nine o'clock to eleven. I hope that will work in your schedule."

"That's during my Psychology class. Is there some way I could get my Psychology class moved to two o'clock in the afternoon?"

"Let me see what I can do." The Dean answered. "Not really, maybe we can turn some of your other classes around." He went through the classes that TJ has and what ones were available in other spots.

"Ah, I think I have the solution. You may have to drop your English class and retake it next semester. That's the best I can do."

"I really don't want to drop English, but I do want to take Culinary I. I'll do it. Can you give me a place next semester for my English class, so it will be locked in?" TJ was trying to be helpful, especially since Dean Danbury was trying so hard to be accommodating for him.

"Yes, you are locked in the place where your swimming class was."

"Thank you so much, Dean. I am grateful for all of your help. When can I start my Culinary I class?"

"Is tomorrow soon enough?" the Dean said jokingly.

"Superb, Sir," TJ said in retaliation also joking. He chuckled as he reached for the Dean's hand and shook it as hard as he could.

TJ went to the library and took the books required for his new class. He was so excited, he was almost giddy.

He returned to his apartment. Joe was waiting for him. "TJ, I have found a new roommate. I will be moving out this weekend. I hope this doesn't upset things too much. I've already paid for this month's rent, so everything should be ok. I realize things will never workout for us. I think my new roommate is my type."

"Joe, I wish you the best of luck. Don't forget to keep in touch. I still regard you as a good friend, even though we don't think the same way. By the way, I start my Culinary I class tomorrow."

"I am so happy for you. Now I hope things will work out between you and Angelica," Joe said sincerely.

"Yes, tomorrow is a big day in my life. I just hope that you will find happiness. You deserve it. You have been a good friend to me."

"May I hug you?" Joe asked.

"Of course," was the answer.

Joe and TJ embraced for a good minute.

TJ remarked, "I will always regard you as one of my best friends."

"Thank you, TJ, you are probably the best straight guy I will ever know," Joe said. "You knew what I was, and yet, you never held it against me. I really thought we had a good thing going, but now I know you are a genuinely good person."

* * * * *

'I wish I could find another roommate. The payments on this place are humongous. I don't know how I will keep going on my small salary. I guess I'll just have to tighten the old belt, 'TJ chuckled to himself. 'I'd better get a good night sleep.'

* * * * *

He had another fretful night sleep. He tossed and turned most of the night. He decided to get dressed and go for a run. He ran to the door of the Gym, but didn't go in. He stood and looked in the window of the door. All was dark. That use to be his favorite place to be. How things can change so quickly. Was Coach Andrews trying to help someone else work into the Olympics? 'He was more excited about the entrance into the Olympics than I was, now that I think about it. I really did love to swim, though.

Maybe I'll go swimming in a public pool this summer. That could be fun, but it will never be the same as practicing to become an Olympian.' He walked back to his apartment. 'Now, I'll have to concentrate on becoming the World's Greatest Chef,' he smiled.

* * * * *

As TJ walked into his new class, he looked carefully around to see if there was anyone he knew. In the middle of the classroom sat Angelica. She looked at him and blushed. There was only one seat empty, so he walked over and sat. He tried not to look at her, but she was so beautiful, he couldn't help staring. He still loved her, he couldn't change that.

* * * * *

Half of the Culinary I class was Theory and the second half was Practical Cooking. The Theory part was boring because he was so far behind. The Practical Cooking was fun, because he did well in that part. During the cooking part he got as close to Angelica as he was able. The Professor paired everyone up and gave instructions on what each pair should cook according to what they were taught in the Theory part.

TJ was paired up with Anthony. Thank Heavens he was top in his class. TJ was thankful he hadn't been put with some ditz that didn't know one end of a spatula from the other.

The dish that he and Anthony got was a relatively easy one. They went together to get the ingredients and took them back to their station. Anthony took the lead and explained to TJ the process. They had thirty-five minutes to complete the project. Each station had a pot of water already boiling. That made it easier since they had a pasta dish. TJ put the pasta into the boiling water along with salt, while Anthony started pealing and cutting the vegetables into bite-size pieces. Then TJ started making the sauce for the vegetables and pasta. Anthony started searing the vegetables in butter. The sauce was perfect. The pasta was a little al denta, but when it was incorporated with the vegetables and sauce, the dish turned out beautiful.

Professor Dana took his time to look each item over carefully. He took a spoon and tasted each dish. When he got to Anthony and TJ's dish, he smiled. He tasted it with a clean spoon, "Men, you have done a splendid job. The pasta was cooked exquisite, the sauce had just the right amount of seasoning, and the vegetables were cooked to perfection. Gentlemen, your dish is superb."

"Tom, I would like to see you after class," Professor Dana announced.

"I hope that is a good thing," he said to Anthony.

Anthony just smiled.

When the class was dismissed, TJ stayed behind per Professor Dana's instructions.

"I see that you have been waiting a while to get into my class," Professor Dana stated.

"Yes, Sir. I have wanted to take Culinary Class for some time. I started cooking with my mother when I was a young child. I decided it was time to start my career as a Chef," TJ answered.

"But you were doing so great on the Swim Team. Why the change?" the Professor asked.

"Yes, but I realized that is not what I would be doing very long. Maybe twenty years at the most. Then what? Run endorsements for swim gear? There has to be more to life than that. And because I learned so much from my mother and loved cooking and baking with her, it seemed natural for me to become the best Chef I am capable of being," TJ smiled at the Professor.

Professor Dana came back with, "I admire your honesty. I can see you are an exceptional young man. Not many students would be so forthright as you." He held out his hand to shake TJ's. "Welcome to the class. I look forward to working with you."

TJ extended his hand to take the Professor's, "Thank you, Sir, I look forward to learning all I can from you."

After the two men shook hands, TJ turned and walked out of the classroom.

* * * * *

TJ was elated. He could tell he was in the right class.

He had to go to work at the Library. He was thankful for the job even though it didn't pay very well. He earned enough to pay for his apartment rent, and a little left for food.

He was also thankful for the Grants that Dean Danbury was able to acquire for him. He knew he would not be able to pay for all of his classes by himself.

At ten o'clock, when his shift was done, his supervisor said she would like to talk to TJ.

'Uh oh, what have I done now?'

"TJ, you have missed quite a few days of work lately. That is unacceptable. I don't want excuses. I just want you to promise that you will be here every day you are scheduled to work. Can you promise me that?" Joanne the head librarian asked.

"Yes, ma'am, I'm sure I have everything straightened out now," TJ said.

"Good. You are a good worker and I need more people like you."

"Thank you, Joanne. I really need this job. I promise I will do my best." He smiled at the woman then turned and walked out the door.

* * * * *

When he got to his apartment there was a note on the door. He peeled it off and entered. He put his books and the note on the table. He was hoping to start catching up in Culinary I theory. He was behind because it was well into the semester and he had missed a lot.

He opened the book and started reading. Then the note that had been left on the door seemed to jump out at him.

He picked it up and just stared. It was hand written by what looked like a woman's handwriting. He knew he should open it, however, he just looked at it mesmerized. Who would leave a note for him on his apartment door? He was dumbfounded. He knew he would never find out if he didn't open it. He put it on the table in front of him and stared. He turned it over and tore open the envelope. It was a message from Angelica.

Dearest TJ, 'That was a pleasant beginning. Dearest? That was almost too good to be true. Maybe it was a fluke.' It went on,

I would like to see you. I think we have some things to discuss. Can we have lunch tomorrow in the cafeteria? 'Is she going to tell me she doesn't want to see me anymore? I would still be in the same class with her. Maybe she means she doesn't want to see me outside of class. Maybe that's it. Then the salutation.' Sincerely, Angelica.

'Sincerely? What does that mean? She sincerely doesn't want to see me? Sincerely, she does? I'm reading too much into a small note. I can see this is going to be another sleepless night.'

He folded the note and put it inside of the book as a bookmark. He tried to read some more of the theory book, but just couldn't digest any of it. They were just a lot of words jumbled together.

He picked up the note and read it over and over until he was too tired to read it anymore.

He shut the note in the book and got his pajamas on and went to bed. To his amazement he fell right asleep and didn't wake up until the alarm sounded its disgusting chime. 'The alarm was still set for 4:00. I don't have to be up until 6:00. Two whole hours. Of course, I couldn't go back to sleep, so I guess I'll study.'

He stayed in his pajamas and opened the book. There was that note. He didn't open it again. He knew what it said.

Theory is always boring, but he must catch up with the class. He is behind about six weeks. That's a lot of catching up to do. Luckily, he retains what he reads easily.

About 7:00, he shaved and took his shower. Then he grabbed a stale donut and ate it and drank a glass of milk. Not exactly a nutritious breakfast, but it will have to do until lunch. Lunch! He almost forgot meeting Angelica for lunch at the cafeteria.

His whole morning was ruined. He tripped over a bump in the sidewalk, stumbled up the stairs, and sat down in the wrong seat. Another student stood and waited for TJ to get out of his seat. How humiliating! The whole class laughed. He felt like crawling in a hole. The Professor was understanding and didn't pick on him, TOO MUCH.

* * * * *

When it was lunch time, he walked to the cafeteria to wait for Angelica. To his surprise, she was waiting for him.

He smiled and greeted the love of his life, "Hi, Angelica." He pointed to an empty chair, "Is this seat taken?"

"I believe I saved that particular chair for you," she said.

"How kind of you," he said jokingly.

"I wanted to talk to you about our situation," the woman said.

"Uh, I didn't know we had a situation," TJ stated.

"Well, maybe we don't. I still think we should talk. The man I have been seeing, has asked me to marry him. I haven't given him an answer yet. I've spent a lot of time thinking about you. How would you feel about my getting married?" she queried.

"I wouldn't mind as long as it was to me." TJ tried to be funny, but that wasn't working. "To be serious, I would be upset. You are the only woman I have ever loved. I would be devastated thinking about you being married to someone else, but if you love him, then, that's what you should do. If he can make you happy, then, you do what you think is best. I can guarantee, one of us will be hurt."

"Jon is a good man. He would be a good husband and father. You on the other hand you are funny. I know you would make me happy. Jon is a Mormon and a returned Missionary. You are not a member. TJ, I am torn. I don't know what to do."

TJ just looked at her and said, "You do what you think is right. A wise woman once told me, 'I cannot make that decision for you. You have to decide who the right one is'."

"That sounds like something your mother would say."

"As a matter of fact, it was she. She's the wisest person I know."

"She made me feel right at home," Angelica remembered.

"She thought you were the greatest thing since vanilla ice cream. The next letter I got from her, she wanted to know when we were going to become engaged. She loves you as if you were her own daughter. I've never seen her so excited about anyone I had brought home before. Of course, you were the first girl I had ever brought home. And the spaghetti put the icing on the cake. That's called teaching the teacher."

"I don't think I have ever felt as welcome as I did at your parent's house," Angelica exclaimed.

"Well, take your time. You don't have to make a decision right now. Don't let anyone pressure you into making a decision. Jon should know the dilemma you are in. But don't let him put you in a place where you have to decide right away. Talk to your parents. Let them know how you feel."

"TJ, I am so glad that we had this talk. I feel so much better. Well, I think I had better get to my next class. Thank you for everything." Angelica reached across the table and gave him a small kiss on the cheek.

As she walked away, he was in a daze. 'She kissed me. I didn't expect that, but I will savor that small moment forever. Wow!'

He went the opposite way to his next class. He had no idea when he would see her again, except in Culinary I. Yes, Culinary class. He could hardly wait. He didn't remember much about his next class, Calculus. Everything was a blur.

When he got to Culinary I, Angelica was already seated. When she saw TJ, she smiled at him. He could feel his heart flutter.

'Will I be the one she will marry or will it be Jon?' He could only hope.

* * * * *

TJ didn't speak to Angelica for quite a while. They were both busy with academics and work. They really didn't have time for anything else. He figured when she was ready to talk, she would let him know.

One day when he saw her in class, there was something shiny on her hand. Oh no, she has decided to marry Jon. It had to be expected. After all, they had more in common. But he loved her. He didn't think she loved Jon. Maybe her parents explained to her that she would be happier with Jon. But, would she. He was sure she loved him, not Jon. He had better ask her after class. He had to know, no matter how devastating it was.

When class was finished, he went directly to her. "Angelica, are you and Jon engaged?"

"No, why do you ask?" Angelica wondered.

"I thought I saw a diamond ring on your finger."

Angelica laughed, "That is my mother's ring. I had admired it so she asked if I would like to wear it. Of course, I said yes."

"Whew! I was afraid you had made up your mind and decided to marry Jon. I am so relieved. I hope I am still in the running," TJ commented.

"Actually, I wanted to talk to you about that," Angelica stated. "I have decided to break up with Jon. He just isn't my type. He's too serious. I want someone with a good sense of humor, that I can laugh with and enjoy life."

"What was your decision, besides getting rid of sober Jon?"

"I have really liked you from the first time we met," Angelica said carefully.

TJ looked at her wondering what she meant, "You liked me? I don't understand. I have been in love with you since the first time I saw you."

"I guess I am a little more careful. I want to take my time to be sure of my feelings," the girl said.

"Well, have you made up your mind? If you do not love Jon and do not want to marry him, who is the lucky guy?" TJ was getting anxious.

Angelica grinned, "You silly. There is no one else I feel I could be happy with. You're smart, you're funny, and you're darn good looking."

She wrapped her arms around his neck and kissed him hard.

"Wow! That was totally unexpected, but I liked it. Let's try that again." This time he grabbed her and planted a kiss. He didn't ever want to let go.

Then TJ stated frankly, "I think we had better tell our parents. Mine will be delighted. Yours, not so much."

"Why do you say that? They haven't even met you yet. They will love you as I do," was Angelica's rebuttal.

"They won't be happy when they find out I'm not a member of your church," TJ said matter-of-factly.

Angelica came back with, "I know they want me to be happy. And I won't be happy with anyone else but you."

"Well, I have to write a letter to my parents. They will be elated. Then we better make arrangements for me to meet your parents," TJ announced.

"I'll make plans for you to meet my parents," as Angelica took TJ's hand and held it with her two.

* * * * *

One peck on the lips and they separated to take care of their tasks.

FOURTEEN

TJ's task was easy, or was it?

Dear Mom and Dad,

I have taken care of everything on my 'To Do List'. I spoke to Coach Andrews. That was difficult. He practically had me signed up for the Olympics next year. When I told him I was going to drop my Swim Team, I thought he was going to cry. He explained how much he had done for me. When I told him I was going to take Culinary I, he laughed. I guess he thought real men didn't go to Culinary School. That was for sissy women. I could have lashed out at him, but instead, I was honest with him.

Next, I saw Dean Danbury about getting into Culinary I. he asked me questions about my reasons for opting out of the Swim Team. I was honest and forthright with him. He said he would try to get me into that class right away. He was pleased with my transcript. It turned out there wasn't anything available for that class. He said he would keep watching to see if anyone decided to quit. He said the class is full at this time.

I got a call to come and see him a week ago. He told me there had been a drop out and I could start on Monday, if I was still interested. Of course, I was.

I spoke to Joe and told him he if he wanted to stay in the apartment, he would have to stay in his own bedroom at night and I didn't want him bringing any of his friends over because I had to do a lot of studying. I was joining the class so late in the semester that I would prefer a quiet atmosphere. He told me today that he was moving in with one of his friends. That will make it hard for me to keep up the rent here unless I can find another roommate.

Last of all, and most important, Angelica and I are going to be married. No date has been set yet. I hope it won't be too long. I know you are as happy about this as I am.

First thing, I have to meet her parents. I hope they like me. I'm still not ready to join any church. I hope they're fine with that.

Well, as you can tell, my life has been anything but uncomplicated. I'm waiting for the roof to fall in at Angelica's house. I don't think they will be agreeable to our marriage. That sounds strange. Marriage, I sure didn't think I was ready for any kind of commitment. I guess I was wrong. We will be out to see you soon.

I love you guys. You are the best parents in the world.

Love,
TJ

* * * * *

Angelica wasn't as happy to tell her parents. She loves TJ, but as he said, he isn't a member of her church. She called her family on the phone, "Hello, Mama? I have something I would like to tell you."

"Hello, Angel, it's so good to hear from you. Is everything ok?" Peggy asked. She had called her daughter Angel since she was old enough to understand the meaning of Angelica.

"Everything is more than ok. I'm engaged to be married."

"Jon will make the perfect husband. I just don't know what took him so long to ask you." The expected conclusion from a parent that hadn't been informed.

"Mother, it isn't Jon. We broke up. It's TJ. Actually, his name is Thomas Allen Williams, Jr. He is called TJ. He is perfect for me."

"Where does he go to Church? Which Temple are you going to be married in?" The next expected questions.

"Mama, he isn't a member of any church, but he is a good man and he has wonderful parents." Now Angelica was making excuses.

"Angelica Marie Murray, how can you even think of marrying outside the Church?" Another expected question.

"Mama, he is wonderful and I know you will love him almost as much as I do."

"You were brought up in the Church and are expected to marry a nice young man in one of our Temples."

"I would like to bring him home right away so you can meet him and get to know him." She had her fingers crossed behind her back.

"Of course, we want to get to know him right away," Peggy was trying to sound enthusiastic.

"Can we come this Saturday?" Angelica was apprehensive.

"I do have a meeting this Saturday, but I will let everyone know I won't be able to make it. This is much more important."

"Thank you, Mama. We will come early so we will have the whole day to become acquainted."

"We will look forward to meeting BJ?"

"No Mama, TJ."

"Oh yes, of course. We will see you Saturday. Bye-Bye, Honey"

"Bye-Bye, Mama. Give Dad and all of my brothers, my love."

"I will, and I'm sure they will all be anxious to meet your young man."

'That was painful, but I knew it would be.'

FIFTEEN

The next day, TJ and Angelica met for lunch in the cafeteria.

"I've made plans to take you to meet my parents," Angelica said.

"Ok, I'm excited to meet them. How did it go?" TJ asked.

"Pure torture. Questions galore. Mama jumped to the conclusion that I was marrying Jon. I explained that Jon and I had broken up. Then she wanted to know what Church you went to and what Temple we were going to be married in. I had to tell her you aren't a member. Then she chastised me for marrying outside the Church."

"When are we going to meet your family?" TJ enquired.

"Early Saturday," was the answer.

* * * * *

Angelica was quiet when TJ opened the car door for her.

"What's wrong, Sweetheart?" TJ interjected.

"I'm scared. I'm afraid you won't like them," the girl said.

"I'm afraid they won't like me. I'm not the kind of guy they want you to marry. I don't meet their criteria."

"They can't help but love you because I do," Angelica reported.

"But I am not a Mormon," TJ reminded her.

"I know." Angelica said wistfully.

"What can I do? What should I say? Are you sure you want to marry me?" TJ was confused.

"Just be yourself. You are wonderful, smart, and funny. You are also genuine."

TJ listened to all Angelica had to say, but he was not convinced. "What if they refuse to let you marry me?"

"I'm a full grown woman. I can make my own decisions."

Silence!

* * * * *

They pulled into Angelica's parents' driveway. TJ walked around the car and opened the door for her and took her hand and helped her out. He stood for a moment and looked at the house. The yard was beautifully manicured. Lovely flowers strategically planted where they would look the best.

He said to his fiancé, "Are you sure we are at the right house? This looks like it should belong to the Governor."

Angelica laughed, "Come on, let's go in." She held his hand and led him through the door.

The whole family was waiting.

Peggy and Gordon were at the head. They were smiling, as if they knew a secret and wouldn't tell anyone.

The parents greeted TJ with big hugs and handshakes.

"TJ, these are my wonderful parents, Peggy and Gordon Murray,"

TJ returned the greetings. "I'm so glad to meet you. I've heard such wonderful things about you." TJ was smiling so much that it could have lit up the whole room.

Matthew asked, "How about us?"

Angelica blushed, "These are my brothers and sister." She pointed to each one and introduced them. "This is Matthew, he's the oldest. Next to him is Joseph. Then Lucas. And my sister is Joanna. Mark is on his mission. He will be home next year in March."

TJ said, "I'm so happy to meet all of you. And I will look forward to seeing Mark next March."

Then the conversation got awkward. No one knew what to say. Finally, Peggy spoke up and said, "Let's sit around the table and talk."

TJ looked relieved, "That sounds like a good idea."

Matthew acknowledged, "I have to be going to work. If I don't leave now, I will be late. See you later, I'll bring Mary and the baby over." He smiled as he exited out the back door.

The other siblings made their excuses and left.

Now all that was left was Mama, Dad, and the two love birds.

"Have you decided on a wedding date, yet?" Peggy inquired.

Angelica decided to answer, "Not yet. We've just become engaged."

TJ sat very quiet and played with his fingernails.

Then it was Dad's turn, "TJ, are you going to join our Church?"

"Not yet, I haven't decided when or even if I will join your Church. I have taken two lessons. I find it very interesting, but I have never belonged to any church."

"We expect Angel to be married in one of the Temples."

"I wouldn't mind being married in a Temple if that is what Angelica wants."

"No one can be married in a Temple unless he or she is a member and holds a Temple recommend."

"What is a Temple recommend?"

"You have to be a member of the Church in good standing," Gordon stated.

"I guess we won't be married in a Temple," TJ related.

Peggy turned to Angelica, "Are you sure you want to marry outside of the Church?"

"I love TJ, member or not."

TJ stated, "I will go to Church with her if she wants me too."

Angelica perked up, "That's good to know. Especially, when we have children." Then she blushed.

Gordon asked, "Where do you plan on getting married?"

Angelica mentioned, "You could marry us, but I would rather have a different Bishop marry us in our Ward building."

TJ looked surprised, "We haven't even got to discussing wedding plans. I'm open to any suggestions."

"We will talk about it privately and come to some decisions," the wife-to-be smiled.

* * * * *

Dinner was a huge success. Roast Beef, potatoes, carrots, and Apple pie for dessert. TJ remarked, "I can see where Angelica learned her love of food and her desire to become a chef. Peggy, dinner was wonderful. My mother is a great cook and so are you."

"Thank you TJ. Let's get to know you a little better. Tell me about your family," Peggy coaxed.

TJ started out slowly, "My family consists of my father Tom, my mother Janet and myself. My father owns a large dairy farm, my mother is a stay-at-home mother. My father worked on the farm most of the time. I stayed in the house with my mother. I learned a great deal from her about cooking, baking, canning, freezing food and keeping a clean house."

Gordon asked, "What about farming? A lot of boys would like to follow in their father's footsteps."

TJ came back with, "I was never interested in farming. My father tried to interest me in his vocation to no avail."

Peggy intervened with, "What about cars and trucks? Most boys like those."

"I was never interested in sports, cars, trucks or anything most boys like. I would rather stay in the house and help my mother or color or read books," TJ reiterated.

"I really feel sorry for my father now. He tried really hard to cultivate me into the best man he could.

"When I was in my teens, I discovered a love for swimming. I had a wonderful high school coach. He pulled some strings and got me into the best college with a great Swim Team and a great swim coach. He was grooming me to be in the Olympics next year. I even got a full four year scholarship."

Gordon said, "You turned that down to go to Culinary School?"

"Yes, I met a wonderful girl. I had never been interested in girls until I met Angelica.

"Also, I discovered I liked cooking more than swimming," TJ snickered.

"I told Angelica I wanted to go to Culinary School so when I was too old to compete in swimming, I would have something to fall back on. Your daughter told me she was taking Culinary I, and things started falling into place. I told my coach that I wasn't going to be on the Swim Team anymore. He laughed when I told him I wanted to go to Culinary School. He thought that was for sissy boys."

"That must have been hard," Peggy said.

"Yes, it was, but I was determined. I went to see Dean Danbury and told him my plans. He was very supportive. He looked over the schedule for

Culinary I and said the class was full. However, he would keep his eyes open, and if anyone dropped out, I could transfer to the class."

Gordon asked, "So you are taking that class now?"

"Angelica and I had gone our separate ways, because I would not join her Church. She was going with Jon. When I saw her in class, I knew I would probably never love anyone else. I knew she was perfect."

"TJ, you are a very interesting young man. You are unconventional. You know what you want and go after it. I admire that quality," Peggy told him.

"Thank you, ma'am, that means a lot to have you say that."

Angelica didn't have anything to add to his repartee, so she just sat and beamed.

* * * * *

Her family didn't like the fact that TJ wasn't ready to jump in the water and be baptized, but they liked him.

It looks like wedding plans will proceed.

TJ and Angelica talked a lot on the way home.

Angelica started, "Well, Honey, you were a great success."

"Even though, I won't convert to Mormonism?" TJ interjected.

"I think because you were so strong about your feelings, Mom and Dad were totally impressed."

"Well, I think we may have a future. Are you ready to set the date? How about tomorrow?" TJ asked.

"That's one of the many things I love about you. Your sense of humor. A lot has to be done to prepare for a wedding," Angelica commented.

"Such as," TJ was baffled. "I thought all we had to do was go to a Justice of the Peace and say 'I do'."

"Oh no, we are going to do this up right. All the Bells and Whistles."

"There you go. We are barely engaged and you are already taking over." TJ was not a little bit serious and Angelica roared with laughter.

"First of all we have to decide on a date that works out, not only for us, but also both sets of parents. This is no laughing matter, we have to be serious."

TJ, still laughing said, "Of course we want our parents there. Who else needs to be invited?"

"Our friends and relatives," Angelica said.

"I don't have any friends and I don't particularly care for my relatives. How about you?" TJ wanted to know.

"Oh come now, your relatives can't be all that bad."

TJ said, "You haven't met my relatives. Boooring. Every time they come over, I head for my room and don't come out. Not even for Dinner."

"TJ, that's pathetic."

"You think that's pathetic, you should see my relatives. There isn't one I would save in a burning fire."

"We'll invite them anyway, just out of curtesy." Angelica was getting a little upset with TJ. But she would try to be civil through this whole conversation.

"You don't have many people outside of your immediate family, do you?" TJ questioned.

"Mormons tend to have large families. My mother came from a family of six children and my dad came from a family of eight children. With all of my aunts and uncles and their families, there has to be over a hundred."

"You're kidding! That makes my family look small. How will we accommodate all of them?" TJ was flabbergasted.

"My family will take care of most of the arrangements," Angelica said softly. She could see TJ was already over whelmed.

"We'll talk more about this later. You need time to think. Oh, one other thing. You will need a Best Man and I have to have a Maid of Honor." Angelica quietly inserted.

"I'm the Best Man and you are the Maid of Honor."

"No, the Best Man is usually your best friend, and the Maid of

Honor should be my best friend. They walk down the aisle together and stand on either side of us as witnesses to the wedding."

"Why do we need witnesses to verify that we are getting married? We know we are getting married. We are the only witnesses necessary. This is getting too complicated."

"We'll discuss it further, later," Angelica muttered.

TJ stopped in front of Angelica's apartment building. He got out and went around the car and opened the door on the passenger side and helped his fiancé out and walked her up to the door. He kissed her good-night and said, "This is all too confusing, but whatever you want, that is what we'll do. I don't know anything about weddings, but I will learn."

"It will be fine. You'll see," she smiled as she opened the door.

TJ got back into the car. Now he really had a lot on his mind. 'Who would be my Best Man? Coach Andrews? Who is my best friend? Do I have a best friend? Joe has always been my best friend, but would he want to be my Best Man at my wedding? I guess the only way to find out is to ask'.

When TJ got home, he went straight to bed. If he had looked around the living room, he would have seen Joe. "I don't appreciate being ignored, when I come to see my best friend."

TJ heard the familiar sound of Joe's voice. He slipped on his robe and followed the sound of his old friend, Joe."

TJ pointed at Joe and said, "Just the man I want to see."

Joe said, "Uh Oh, now what have I done?"

"I have become engaged, and I would like you to be my Best Man."

"You're kidding me. I am the last person you should ask to be your Best Man. I wanted to be THE MAN."

TJ looked him square in the face, "That would never happen. We could never be lovers. You know I have always loved Angelica. There's no place in my heart for her and you. However, you are my best friend, and I would like you to be my Best Man at my and Angelica's wedding."

Joe threw his arms around TJ's neck and hugged him, "You betcha. I would love to be the Best Man at your wedding. Thank you for asking me. I would have felt bad if you had asked someone else."

"You will always be my best friend." TJ was sincere.

"We can talk tomorrow. Right now, I need my sleep," TJ told Joe.

"Can I sleep on your couch?"

"What happened?"

"We'll talk some more in the morning. You need your sleep."

TJ smiled and headed once more for his bedroom.

* * * * *

He slept well. However, he has a recurring dream. It's not a nightmare, but he doesn't understand it. In it he is in a forest with lots of animals of different kinds. He loves them all and they love him and follow him everywhere. He has always loved all variety of beasts. This dream started when he was very young. He needs to know what all of this means.

* * * * *

TJ woke up invigorated. It had been quite a while since he has had a good-night sleep. It was Sunday. There wasn't anything different about today.

He got up and walked around in his pajamas. He figured he would lounge around all day.

He wouldn't call Angelica until later in the afternoon. He was sure she would be in church at least part of the day.

The phone started ringing. 'Who would call me Sunday morning? He didn't have anything to do. He was planning on laying around and watching a horror flick on the tube.

"Hello? Oh hi, Sweetheart. What's up? I figured you would be in Church sometime today, so I wasn't planning on calling you until later in the afternoon. Uh, after Church?"

"Me go to Church with you? I'm sure I haven't any of the proper clothes to wear, unless they accept jeans and t-shirts."

Angelica told him to come to her parents' house. Matthew will be there with the clothes he should wear.

'Great, so much for my staying here and relaxing.'

"Okay, Sweetheart, I'll be there about 9:00. See you then. I love you. Good-bye."

"How do I get myself into messes like this," he said out loud.

From the other side of the couch, Joe popped up, "That's just the way you are. Sometimes you are just too nice."

"You know me too well."

"Well, it's getting late. I had better go over to Angelica's parents' house. I don't know when I will be back. Make yourself at home."

* * * * *

'This should be interesting. I'm going to some people's house I barely know. I'll be wearing clothes, I don't know if they will even fit me.'

Angelica was at the door waiting for TJ. He asked her, "What am I doing here?"

She looked at him thoughtfully and said, "You are going to Church with me today. Any questions? Good. Follow Matthew. He has some clothes that are appropriate for Church."

'I had a lot of questions, but I didn't want to overwhelm her the first time I have ever been to any church.'

Matthew must have been in a closet for a long time. "Here is a white shirt and tie and black pants." TJ started changing his clothes.

The pants were a little tight. The shirt and tie were fine. "Do men in your Church always have to wear this kind of clothes."

"That is appropriate. If you wanted to wear jeans and a tee shirt they wouldn't kick you out. But if you wear these, you won't feel out of place."

These are way out of my realm.

"Well, at least, people won't look at you funny," Matthew said.

"No, but I sure feel funny, and not in a laughing way."

Angelica came into the room, "You look like a real Mormon".

"Humph!" was the only reply TJ could come up with."

"It's about time to leave," Angelica remarked.

"What about your Dad? I haven't seen him yet". TJ asked.

"Oh, he's been there for hours. He has a meeting first thing in the morning," was Angelica's answer.

"Holy cow, do you ever get to see him?" was TJ's next question.

"Not too often. He's a very busy man," the girl said with a smile.

"TJ, do you want to ride with the family, or would you like to take your car?" Peggy inquired.

"I think Angelica and I will go in my car. That way I can make a quick exit if things don't go well," TJ smirked. He was trying to be funny, but that wasn't going so well.

Peggy said, "Let's go. We don't want to be late."

TJ opened the car door for his fiancé. Then she said, "Oh, there's something I neglected to tell you."

He got in the car and started the engine. "What did you forget to tell me?"

"Um, there are two meetings today. We go to Sunday School in the morning. Then we go back for what is called Sacrament Meeting in the evening."

"Do we have to go to both? I would think once on Sunday would be enough."

"That's the way it is done. In Sunday School we learn about the Bible. This year we are studying the New Testament. The Bible is in two sections, The Old Testament about the beginning of time until the time of Jesus' birth. The New Testament is about the ministry of Jesus. It's very interesting."

"Okay, what about, what is it called? Sac something."

"Sacrament Meeting. In that meeting, people get up and talk about things they have learned or personal experiences that has happened to them. That is very interesting too. Also the sacrament is passed to the members. That's bread and water."

"I think this is too much for me to take in at one time. Why would you go twice to church on Sunday?"

"To learn. We are never too old to learn about the Bible. It's amazing the things you can learn, even if you have been a member all of your life."

"I'll give it a try, just for you." TJ was perplexed.

* * * * *

TJ went through Sunday School, dinner and Sacrament Meeting and then he went back to the apartment.

Joe was still there. "Well, how did it go?"

"What?" TJ asked.

"Is the wedding still on, or have you changed your mind?"

"The wedding is still on. I love Angelica too much to give up because of one day at her church."

"By the way, why are you still here?

"My partner and I had an argument, so I moved out. I knew I could depend on you for a sleep-over. I'll look for another place tomorrow. If you don't mind, I'll sleep on the couch again tonight," Joe said.

"Nah, that's fine. You are still my best friend."

TJ stated, "It's been a long day. I think I'll watch a good Sit-Com and then I'll be off to slumber land."

"I'll be up early. I have a paper due in the morning. I don't need Prof mad at me. He isn't very forgiving," TJ said knowingly.

CHAPTER
SIXTEEN

Wedding plans were complicated, but moving right along. The two love birds talked to Bishop Johnson. He would officiate at the wedding in Angelica's church building. The building is called a Ward.

Bishop Johnson spoke to TJ alone and asked some rather personal questions, like, "Are you planning on joining the Church? Do you drink or smoke? Are you morally clean?"

TJ hesitated with the last question. "I haven't any immediate plans to join any church. I don't drink or smoke. I trained for the Olympics just recently. So no drinking any alcohol or smoking anything."

"What Olympic category were you training for?" Bishop Johnson was curious.

"Swimming. And there was a scout that had been watching me and said he thought he had a couple of companies lined up that might be interested in endorsing me. That is quite an honor,"

"Yes, it is. Why did you decide to quit the Swimming Team and go into the culinary field?" the Bishop asked.

TJ answered, "I grew up helping my mother in the kitchen. I really enjoyed it. I think I knew that someday I would be using the Food Industry as a career."

"As to the question, am I morally clean, I can answer that with a resounding, YES."

"Young man, I find you very worthy to marry Angelica. In fact, I would feel it a privilege to officiate in that ceremony." The Bishop reached for TJ's hand to shake it. TJ grabbed Bishop Johnson's hand with both of his and shook it firmly.

* * * * *

TJ joined Angelica in the foyer and held hands as they walked out to the car.

They decided it was time to set a date for the wedding. "I think June 21st would be a good date. That's the first day of summer," Angelica announced.

"June 21st it is. That would be the third Saturday of June. It's a date," TJ agreed.

"Let's go to my parents and let them know." TJ coaxed.

"That's a fine idea. Then I will call my parents when I get back to my apartment," Angelica said.

* * * * *

As they pulled into the driveway, Tom heard the car and wondered who would be visiting them on a Sunday afternoon.

"Hi kids. What's happening? We didn't expect you today."

"When we get into the house with you and Mom together, we have an announcement to make."

When Janet saw the two lovebirds, she gave both of them a big hug.

"What's up? We weren't expecting you," Mom said.

"We've set our wedding date," TJ smiled.

"Well, what is it?" Both parents said at the same time.

"June 21st, TJ said excitedly.

"Where are you going to have the ceremony?" Mom inquired.

"It will take place in Angelica's Church. One of the Bishops will perform the ceremony," TJ exclaimed.

"Does it have to be in a church? We could have it here. I think we have enough room."

"There will be about one hundred and fifty invitations sent out. Maybe more. That's just relatives. That's not including friends."

"Wow!" was the remark from Tom. We don't have that many relatives."

"No, but Angelica comes from a large family," was the answer from TJ.

"I know we couldn't accommodate that many people. We will need a church. Congratulations, you two. That's only a few months away."

"We know. We have a lot to accomplish in a short amount of time. Angelica hasn't informed her parents of the date yet. She will call them when she gets back to her apartment. I wanted to tell you two right away."

TJ's parents smiled and gave the couple a big hug.

"We are so happy for you. We want to help anyway we can." TJ's mother informed them.

"I'm sure my parents will include you in all of the arraignments,"

"We need to get back now so Angelica can call her parents," was TJ's remark.

"I'm sure you can at least stay for a piece of Chocolate Cream Pie," Janet coaxed.

TJ anxiously replied, "You know I will never turn down a piece of Chocolate Cream Pie.

Angelica nodded in agreement.

Janet quickly prepared two pieces of pie for TJ and Angelica.

Tom looked sad, "What about me?"

"You already had a piece earlier."

"Yes, but I can always eat another." Tom pouted.

TJ and Angelica snickered.

* * * * *

Everyone ate their pie, and TJ and Angelica were on their way back to their apartments. As soon as Angelica was in her apartment, she was on the phone, talking to her mother. "We have set the date for our wedding. June 21st."

"I'm glad you set the date. That's only three months away. We will have to get started with the arrangements right away. You and TJ go to the Hallmark store and pick out an invitation you both like and have the manager mark the one you chose and I will be in tomorrow and order one hundred and seventy-five, and have them engraved. I'll have to have TJ's proper name and his parents first and last name."

Angelica asked, "Will they have time to engrave that many invitations?"

"I'm sure they will. I'll bet they have couples that order Invitations sooner than that, "Peggy told her daughter.

"TJ's name is Thomas Allen Williams, II, His father's name is Thomas Allen Williams, I. His mother's name is Janet, no middle name. That's all I know."

"That will be fine. I'll give them the information so they can get started right away. Oh, are we having a dinner afterwards?"

TJ and I haven't discussed that yet. Go ahead and have the engraving put on. I know TJ will approve."

* * * * *

TJ wrote a letter to his Mom and Dad:

Dear Mom and Dad,

I think I'll come out for a visit this weekend. I thought maybe we could go over our wedding plans. We have accomplished quite a lot since we were out to your house.

I'll be there on Saturday morning, if that is ok.

I will go back to my apartment Saturday night. I plan on going to church with Angelica Sunday morning and evening.

See you soon.

Love,
TJ

* * * * *

He thought he should tell Angelica of his plans. "I am going to my parent's house to let them know of the plans we have made, so far."

"That sounds like a good idea. Would you like me to go with you?"

"I'd love to have you come, but I would like to spend a few hours with just them. I haven't been alone with them for quite a while."

"Ok Darling, but I will miss you." Angelica responded.

"I'll be back Saturday night, so I can go to church with you Sunday."

Angelica was thrilled, "Then I'll see you Sunday morning. I love you."

"I love you too, and I can hardly wait for Sunday. I will miss not seeing you until then," TJ said.

SEVENTEEN

Early Saturday morning TJ got in his car and headed toward his parents' house.

It was a beautiful day. Not a cloud in the sky. 'I miss Angelica already. Oh well, I will see her tomorrow at church. Right now, I feel I need to talk to my mom and dad. I don't want them to feel they are not an important part of our wedding.'

'Dad is probably out with the cows by now. I wish I had been a better son. I should have paid more attention to him when he wanted me to learn about how to run a dairy farm.

I'm glad that I am taking culinary classes in College. I really love to cook and with Angelica in the class with me, we can learn together. I love that aspect.

'The sun is really bright. I can hardly make out what's ahead of me. I'm almost there, I'd better slow down.'

Suddenly, he was in the wrong lane and a car was speeding toward him.

The other car sounded his horn several times, but TJ couldn't see him or anything else.

"Uh oh, too late." He hit the oncoming car.

Everything went blank.

The next thing he knew he was in an ambulance with the siren blaring.

Beside him was a paramedic taking his vitals.

"What happened?" TJ questioned.

"You were in an accident." Replied the man.

"How did that happen? The patient enquired.

"I don't know," was the answer.

"I have to get to my parents' house. They are expecting me," TJ stated.

The attendant answered, "You're going to the hospital. We should be there in about ten minutes."

"No, you don't understand. I'm expected at my parents' house."

"No, you don't understand. You are going to the hospital. You've been injured."

A voice came over the intercom, "John, how is our patient?"

TJ didn't like the response, "I think he's hallucinating."

The voice came back, "Just try to keep him calm."

"You said I was in an accident. Was anyone else involved?"

"Yes, you hit another car head-on."

"Was anyone else hurt?" TJ wondered.

"I can't tell you."

By the time we got there, another ambulance had taken someone else to the hospital.

"Try not to talk. Your blood pressure is climbing."

"My family and my fiancé need to be notified."

"You can give that information when we get you to the hospital."

* * * * *

When they arrived at the hospital, they proceeded to get TJ on to a gurney.

TJ started yelling, "I CAN'T MOVE. HELP ME, WHAT'S WRONG."

"Calm down Mr. Williams. A doctor will be in to see you soon."

He was taken to what looked like a cubical with curtains all the way around. He waited for a doctor to come and see him. Instead, in came a nurse to take his vitals again. When she was finished she announced, "Dr. Jameson will be in as soon as he can."

"What about my family? They need to be notified of my accident."

Nurse Nora asked, "Can you give me a telephone number? I will call them right away."

TJ rattled off the number and Nora smiled and said she would let them know.

"Thank you, you are the kindest person I've seen."

He lay in and out of conciseness until the Doctor came in.

"Well Tom, how are you feeling?"

"My father is Tom, I'm TJ. We are both Tom, but I'm junior. But I go by TJ."

"I'll remember that. Nurse Nora is phoning your parents now."

"Thank you." And TJ passed out again.

* * * * *

When he woke up again, he had tubes in his nose, his leg was bandaged and being suspended from a harness. One of his arms was wrapped and his head was also wrapped. He knew he looked a mess. At least he could see.

The first people he saw were his parents'. His mother was leaning over him and looking at all of the apparatus.

"Mom, I'm going to be all right. It looks worse than it is."

"Does Angelica know?" TJ asked.

"I'm right here, Darling," she answered.

"Get my clothes. I want to get out of here. We have a wedding to plan," the patient demanded.

"You won't be able to go home for some time. You're pretty broken up. You need many operations to put Humpty Dumpty back together again," Mom teased.

"I'm fine. I don't feel any pain." He remarked.

At that moment, Doctor Jameson came in. "Young man, you are lucky to be alive. You had a bad accident. You have many broken bones. We are waiting for an Orthopedic Surgeon to come in."

"What about the other car. Is that person going to make it?" TJ questioned.

"I'm sorry. She didn't make it. She was six months pregnant. Neither made it." Doctor Jameson said almost in a whisper.

TJ had tears running down his face, "I'm so sorry. The sun was in my eyes and I couldn't see."

He looked at the Physician and said, "I will be able to walk down the aisle on my wedding day, won't I?"

"When is the wedding?" Doctor Jameson inquired?

"June 21st. TJ answered proudly.

"I can't say you will ever walk again, Son," Announced Doctor Jameson.

"What do you mean? I have to walk. I have a life ahead of me with a beautiful wife and hopefully beautiful children. I can't be crippled the rest of my life," trumpeted TJ.

Angelica said to TJ, "I will always be with you. Through thick or thin, through sunshine or rain. You are my hero. You can always do whatever you want. I love you with all my heart and soul."

"I will come out of this with my head held high and my spirit soaring. Love Me For Who I Am."

"TJ, we all love you no matter what, because we know you have greatness within you. You will come out of this even better than you've ever been," his mother said through tears. And she meant it.

"I love you all. You are the strength I need to get through this. Now, please go home. I need some time alone to reflect on where I am and where I am going."

"Angelica, we will get through this together." The tears were flowing from all who were in attendance. "All we need is our love."

* * * * *

When the Orthopedic Doctor saw TJ, he ordered x-rays. He was in bad shape. He was going to need many major surgeries. All of the doctors and nurses said they were surprised he lived. He had multiple breaks. And he had a severe concussion. There wasn't hardly a spot on his whole body that wasn't wrapped.

He wasn't in pain because he was heavily sedated.

* * * * *

He had a lot of visitors. All of his relatives, Aunts and Uncles, and a lot of cousins who were old enough to visit in the hospital. It seemed like he didn't have a quiet minute to himself. If family wasn't there, the doctors and nurses were. He knew he was going to be fine. He was determined.

* * * * *

"What about my wedding? Will I be able to limp down the aisle? He asked one of the many surgeons, jokingly.

"I wouldn't worry about that now. First we have to get you better. Then you will have to have Physical Therapy to get your movement back in your body."

"How long will I have to be all wrapped up like this, Dr. Holmes?"

"I can't give you a time. A lot depends on how well you do with your Physical Therapy. Your attitude depends a lot on how quickly you will recuperate, TJ.

The doctor tried to bolster his spirits so he would know that he has to do everything the doctors tell him to do.

"Doctor Holmes, how long do you think it will be before I can walk again? TJ queried.

"Son, I have to be truthful with you. I don't know if you will ever walk again. Your body is all broken up. You have already had multiple surgeries and you will need many more, in my opinion."

TJ thought to himself, 'I will walk. I will walk. You'll see.'

Doctor Holmes left the room.

Tears were running down TJ's face. He couldn't imagine never walking again, or being confined to a wheelchair the rest of his life. He had been looking forward to fulfilling his life with Angelica and children and becoming the best chef in the world. How was he supposed to live like a cripple? He had to get better. He had to be able to use all of his muscles and limbs. He couldn't expect Angelica to marry him this way.

* * * * *

Angelica came to see him right after work. It was late, but the doctors said to let him see anyone, anytime.

"Hi Darling, I hope you are feeling a little better," She smiled at him and bent down to give him a kiss.

He ignored her. He didn't want to see her or anyone.

"What's the matter? Don't you want me here?"

"No, go away. The doctor said there is a possibility that I will never walk again. I won't marry you to put you through a life of taking care of a cripple."

"TJ, I told you I would stay with you through thick or thin. Believe me, you will never get rid of me. I will always love you and be by your side forever."

"Get out! I don't want you to ever see me like this again. How could I expect you to marry me under these conditions? TJ continues: "I won't, no, I won't put you through a life of taking care of an invalid. You are young and beautiful and deserve better than me."

"I will stay with you forever. Don't treat me as if you don't love me. I know you do," Angelica yelled at him. "I'm not marrying an invalid. I'm marrying the man I love. You will get better. You will have a wonderful life as a chef, and we will have many children. You can't give up. I won't let you."

"Angelica, leave. I don't want to see you anymore."

"You're just going through a depression. You need to come out of these feelings you are having," his wife-to-be offered. "I will go home tonight and pray for you. You mustn't give up. You have friends and relatives that love you, and most of all you have me, whether you like it or not. You can't give up. You have too much to live for.

"I'm going to kiss you goodnight and l will see you tomorrow after work. I want you to think about positive attributes tonight. I want you to have a change of attitude by the time I get back."

She bent down and gave him a kiss on a place on his face that didn't have a bandage.

$$* * * * *$$

TJ was being brought back to his room after a lengthy surgery. He was still under the anesthetic he had been given.

The doctor came into the room where his mom and dad were waiting.

"I think this surgery was very successful," said the surgeon.

"Why do you say that, Doctor Keneday?" Janet asked.

"I don't want to get your hopes up, but I thought I saw a slight movement when his bandages were being put on."

"How long do you think it will be before he comes out of the anesthetic?"

"It should be anytime," Doctor Keneday hoped.

Janet and Tom sat for a long time. Anyway, it seemed that way.

Then suddenly, out of the corner of her eye, she thought she saw a little twitch in TJ's hand. She was startled. This time she stared at his hand. Again, she was sure she saw it twitch. She looked at Doctor Keneday. He had seen it too.

TJ awoke. "That feels strange."

Doctor Keneday asked, "What feels strange?"

"It felt like my hand moved."

"We all saw it. Your hand twitched. You are making remarkable strides. It won't be too long and you will be walking," the doctor teased.

"That's not funny. Now I know I will be getting better. No more negativity. I WILL WALK. I will be the person I am supposed to be once again".

"Where is Angelica? I have to tell her about my latest operation."

Angelica quietly sneaked into TJ's room. She didn't know if he would want to see her or not.

Janet saw her and motioned for her to come closer. "He has something he would like to tell you."

All she could think of was that he wanted to break up with her. She couldn't bear the thoughts of being without him.

She quietly moved closer, until he could see her.

"Come close, Sweetheart, I want to talk to you."

She went closer, but hesitantly.

"I love you and I would like to get married right away. I know I will get better. Watch me move my hand."

"Darling, that is wonderful. I always knew you would completely recover. I will get in touch with Bishop Johnson and make arrangements to have a wedding with just our parents here."

TJ said, "That is what I have always wanted."

* * * * *

Bishop Johnson came in TJ's room, "Well, I hear we are going to have a wedding here soon."

"Yes, Sir, I am going to have a full recovery. I had a dream that started when I was a little boy. I've had that dream over and over. I finally figured out what that dream might mean."

"Tell me about it," the Bishop coaxed.

"Ok", TJ started. "I was in a forest with a lot of animals of different kinds. I loved them and they followed me around all the time. That was the end of the dream."

"What do you think that means?" the Bishop asked.

"I think I am supposed to help people. All kinds of people. I'm not sure how I am supposed to help them, but I do know that I love all kinds of people. I don't care what color they are, where they came from, or anything peculiar about them. If they need help of any kind, I will do anything I can for them. But first Angelica and I want to get married. While I am recovering, I will help everyone I can. Does that make sense?"

"It sure does. I think you have found your calling in life. But what does that have to do with the food industry?"

"Maybe I will help people learn how to cook, bake and anything else they want to learn," TJ said with pride. "I figured I could be a famous Chef. Possibly, this is the way I will be able to help others."

"It's a beautiful idea. I'll help any way I can", was the kind offering of the Bishop.

"Well, first of all, let's get you kids married", was the gesture. "When can we get that accomplished?"

TJ said, "As soon as possible. Let's plan a date and time. I know we will have both sets of parents here. That's all we need, except for a marriage license. Angelica and my Mom can take care of that."

Bishop Johnson smiled, "How about next Saturday at 1:00 pm?"

"That sounds good to me. I'll get in touch with Angelica. She can arrange it with her parents and I will set it up with my parents. That will be perfect." TJ smiled.

* * * * *

Saturday was a beautiful day. The sun was shining and there was a slight warm breeze. TJ had the nurse open the window just a little bit.

Janet and Peggy came early and decorated the best they were able. Janet made the cake. TJ thought everything looked perfect.

The Bishop was there about ten minutes early to make sure the license was in order.

At 1:00 sharp, Peggy turned the record player on to the Wedding March.

Angelica came into the room in a beautiful, long white wedding gown. Tears came to TJ's eyes. Angelica looked more beautiful than she ever had. She stood by TJ's bed and held his hand.

Bishop Johnson performed the ceremony. It couldn't have been any better. When he stated, "You may now kiss the bride." Angelica bent down and kissed her husband. It was perfect. Everything had gone on without a hitch.

9 781959 365006